SAFE WORD

CHARLOTTE BARNES

BLOODHOUND
— BOOKS —

ALSO BY CHARLOTTE BARNES

BEFORE

I hadn't expected him to be the cheap lead in a paperback romance. And yet, everything about the situation now spoke of melodrama. When I'd agreed to go home with him, I'd hoped to be swinging from the rafters; fingers knotted in hair and breath snatched clean out of me with the heat of it all. But instead, he was preparing for what looked more like a laughable re-enactment of something from a soft porn film – and not an especially good one at that. He dimmed the lights and queued a string of atmospheric instrumental tracks on the sound system, then set about lighting a collection of candles that made a circuit around the room. I sighed, and he must have heard the disappointment in it.

'Did you think I'd rip your clothes off as soon as we walked through the door?' He turned, blew the match out and dropped it in a nearby ashtray. 'I somehow thought you'd appreciate a more gentlemanly approach than that.'

I laughed. 'Why?'

He landed hard on the sofa alongside me. But he leaned forward to grab his drink as he answered, which shielded his face from view. 'I thought you had more substance.'

The comment cut me; I guessed it was meant to.

'I'm not sure hurting a girl's feelings is the best way to get her into bed.'

He swallowed so deeply that I heard the gulp of his drink go down. 'What makes you think I'm trying to get you into bed, Agnes?'

It felt like a second slash; a sharp blade gently piercing the skin, just enough to draw blood. After months of flirting, I'd been hoping for more than schoolboy antics to offend me, presumably as a ruse to make me more interested. If anything, it was having the opposite effect.

'Look–'

He put his hand flat over my mouth and stifled the excuse I was about to make to leave. In a swift move, he snatched his hand away and kissed me instead. The force of the gesture set me back against the headrest of the sofa. My neck bent back at an uncomfortable angle and the weight of him pressed against me felt odd, awkward. But nothing in me wanted it to stop.

When he eventually pulled away, he laughed lightly, the huff of it falling against my lips before he righted himself and said, 'It's not that I don't *want* to take you to bed, you understand that?'

I narrowed my eyes and searched his expression. There was a clue here to understanding him, if only I could ferret through the cloak folds long enough to find it. He was the one who'd initiated this, after all, and I refused to believe he'd brought me home with only candles, warm wine and soft insults in mind.

'Why am I here?' I asked eventually, when the knot of nerves gave way to something more like irritation, impatience.

He fidgeted about and opened his mouth once, twice before he managed to answer. 'Agnes, why do you think I asked you about a safe word?'

CHAPTER ONE

I wear the name 'wife' in the same way I wear my engagement ring – with a pinch and a fake smile. That's how he introduces me to people: 'my wife'. I am a nameless creature rolled out at business events and then shuffled home in a chauffeured car, to the two-storey cottage with an impeccable front garden; a landscape minded by a young and clichéd handsome man from two villages over. He comes and he tends and I pay him – because horticulture is one of many areas in which I have failed. But in being wife I am impeccable: conventionally attractive; astute enough to laugh at the right jokes; mostly quiet with my opinions. If someone were to shake me, I sometimes worry at the things that would come tumbling out.

'Agnes?' He clicked his fingers in front of my face. 'Are you ready?'

'Do we really have to go to this, Fin?' I kept a look out of the window as I spoke. Dermot and Xara were having an argument right there on their front lawn and I thought if I paid close enough attention I'd stand a chance of lip-reading their dispute.

I sighed: *This is what I'd been reduced to.* When Fin and I met, I was better than this. I was–

'You're not listening to me.' He turned me roughly, one finger under my chin to yank my face. 'Yes, we have to go. Yes, you need to show up for me. This company has put a lot of money into the department, and you know what that means.' With a finger still pressed to my chin, he guided my head into a nod. *Yes, Finian. No, Finian. Three bags–* 'There will be some of the old lot there, so you'll have someone to talk to. A few of them are married off themselves now.' He let me go, then, and crossed to the large mirror on the other side of the bedroom. 'It'll be good for you to mix with others.'

When he says 'the old lot', he means people I used to work with. Finian and I studied for our doctorate degrees at the same university. Mine, English literature; his, geography. Our earliest years together were spent arguing over the relevance of each subject and now, given that he was a working lecturer and I was a housewife with no family to nurture, it felt as though the final dig of the argument had been made. I sometimes wondered whether that's why he'd relegated me to being this angel of his house; to prove a point.

Sometime during our second year of study, we started to have sex in every corner of the campus. Sometime during our teacher training – also together – he proposed. I was young and whimsical enough to believe it was a good idea; too much time with my head spent in books, my mother might have said. Still, when I make a decision I stick to it, and that applied to the engagement, the wedding and now, this, our blissful, glossy marriage. Six months after the wedding was when Fin dropped the bombshell, though – 'Why do you even *need* to work?' – and whenever I provided him with ammunition of a difficult day in the classroom, an avalanche of marking, the *endless* inter-department emails, he would boomerang them back to me and dangle the proverbial carrot: 'Don't you want an easier life, sweetheart? A life away from it all?' He was on a full-time contract by then while I was a fractional worker; in one classroom for half the week and another for the rest. He could afford to carry us for a while; that was the party line he eventually won with. The suggestion that this would be temporary; that one day, I might be a three-dimensional working-woman again. Only soon, children were mentioned; trying for a family: 'Doesn't it make sense that *you'd* stay home with them?'

We don't yet have children. And on my worst days I imagine the mustard wallpaper in the would-be nursery might be housing a mirror image of myself who lives in the pattern. If that happens to be true, I hope her life is a damn sight more exciting.

He was still looking at himself, straightening his tie, when I said, 'You look good.' This was my expected line. And I delivered it with such conviction that he cocked an eyebrow at his reflection, straightened his tie again, and shrugged as though double-checking the fit of his blazer. It fit perfectly, of course. Fin's measurements are something I know by heart; my recall is great for 'important' information like that. When he didn't answer I added, 'I would.'

His head snapped up, then, and he stared at me through the looking glass. 'We don't have time, Agnes.'

I walked over and wrapped my arms around him until my hands settled on his hips. My chin rested neatly on his shoulder, such was our convenient height difference – and my strategic use of the lowest kitten heels available. He was looking at me in the mirror still, but I kept my eyes hooded beneath glittered lids. 'You're the boss.'

I heard him huff out a near-laugh, and I knew he must be smiling.

This was also my expected line.

There were people waiting with red and white offerings when we arrived outside the venue. If I'd been from the donating company, I'd wonder how many of the bottles I'd paid for versus how many sites of historic and geographic interest I'd helped to discover. *But what do I know?* I took a glass of white for me, red for Fin; he hated the taste but he thought the colour looked better on him.

On the journey to the hall Fin had coached me on the people to look out for; those from his department – as though I were a rookie – and those from outside the department. Apparently one of the donors was known for being hard to get close to but Fin seemed determined, and said, 'You were always good at breaking down walls whenever someone new came into the fold. Use your natural charms, okay?' He tapped my arse lightly then held his arm up for me to loop a hold of. The room was swamped by people eager to impress and be impressed, and I was already calculating the likely timescale for our escape. *We should have decided on a safe word.* Still, at least if academia went in for centrefolds, we would have been first pick in the place; just how Fin liked it.

'Dr and Mrs Villin, a joy to have you here as always.'

Dr and Dr. 'Jim, always a pleasure, never a chore.' I let him kiss my cheek while I fixed a smile in place just in time for when he backstepped from me. 'I'm still clinging onto that doctorate for dear life, though, and don't you forget it.' I winked.

'You're no longer teaching?' The question came from a woman I didn't know: petite; pretty; she wasn't wearing a wedding ring. *He hasn't mentioned you...*

'Agnes decided to take some time off,' Fin leapt in.

'Stressful, isn't it, the teaching malarkey?' He looked around the tight group for support and there came a grumble of it. Then, in such a presumptuous gesture that only an entitled male would dare to make it, he set the palm of his hand flat against the round of my belly and said, 'Besides, we're hoping there'll be good reason for her to stay at home soon.'

'Congratulations!' The same woman as before burst out with such an excitement, and in that second I thought: *Be careful with that attitude, dear, because the wolves will get you.*

My smile pulled tight. 'Fin is looking to the future. We're not there, yet.'

'The trying isn't the worst thing in the world, though, is it?'

'Trust you, Philip, Christ.'

'It's not an old boys' brigade here anymore, or did you not get the memo?'

'Oh, I likely got it; but it's buried under twenty others.'

There was a chorus of laughter, then, as though Philip had made the comedy crack of the century. I side-eyed Fin and saw his teeth glint; lips parted in a snarl of amusement. The conversation that followed washed over me. It was part of my housewifery skillset to arrange my face into something that looked like I was actively listening, but it wasn't until I heard my name that I tuned back in.

'I'm just going to aim Agnes at him.'

'At who, sorry?' I asked.

'The donor, sweetheart.'

'Denis Miracle,' Jim filled in the blank of the man's name. 'And don't think we haven't made our fair share of jokes about that around the office.'

'Welsh, I believe,' I said before a sip of wine. Jim's eyes spread in surprise and I laughed as I lowered my glass. 'Don't be so surprised, Jim, they don't take the knowledge out of your head when you leave academia. Language still exists.' I felt Fin

7

tighten his grip around my hand and I knew I'd gone too far. 'Besides, where else will I use these silly words if not for impressing the most attractive geography department this side of the equator?'

Fin loosened his hold then, as though to say, *Yes, that's more like it.* 'Sweetheart, why don't we do a lap and find Denis?' he suggested.

I spent the rest of the evening flirting – just enough, but not too much – with anyone Finian pointed me at. In losing my worth among the latest literary debates, my worth had been replaced, instead, with my ability to make people part with their money – and/or their senses. But by the time the driver was collecting us for the journey home, Fin was smiling and sighing in a way that marked a job well done (on my part), so I knew the talents hadn't failed me. We didn't try for idle conversation, only looked out of our respective windows and kept our hands clasped in the centre seat between us. It wasn't until the city was a safe distance behind us that I asked, 'Who's the woman?'

'Dr Loughty. Irene.'

I noted that he knew exactly who I meant. But I only answered, 'I see.'

CHAPTER TWO

I stood at the window and watched Fin leave. He told me he'd be late home from work because of a staff meeting, following the big benefit bash the week before. I cherished these moments when he cared enough to lie to me – and when I cared enough to believe him. I'd acquiesced as though I were disappointed and promised dinner in the oven, home-cooked (by someone), and ready for him.

'Don't wait up,' he'd said, 'I might hit the gym afterwards if there's time.'

I would spend the morning thinking about the sweat he'd leave for me to wash off his clothes when he came home. After he left, I took my first tea of the day in the living room window. I saw Dermot and Xara leave then, too, holding hands and talking without a force. Although their recent arguments were still written across Xara's face; laughter lines replaced by worry. She kissed his cheek and saw him into the car, then backstepped to the house as he pulled away. Xara was another member of the non-working club. I remained convinced that I'd once seen her trimming the lawn of their front garden to an exact length with a pair of household scissors, and I wondered when she'd last had an orgasm.

Hardly a minute had passed on her closing the door when my mobile chirped.

'Hi, beautiful,' I answered, and I thought I heard Xara blush through the speaker.

'Ag, you old charmer–'

'Less of the old,' I cut her off. 'This is an early call?'

There was a long pause. 'Do you fancy tea?'

Ah, so she's ready for share-time. 'I'll never turn down tea. Your place or mine?'

'Nicole's?'

Fuck. 'Is it a mother's meeting that we're having?'

'God, I hope so, I could do with a good moan.'

My lips thinned to hold in a laugh. I couldn't shake the orgasm idea. 'Nicole's it is, then. What time shall I pop over?'

I took a spiteful amount of pride in making myself look faultless whenever I saw these women. *Because what else am I spending my time on?* Xara took an embarrassing pride in her front garden while Nicole would no doubt have whipped up something from spare ingredients she just happened to have lying around. I clamped my mouth on a tissue to rid myself of excess lipstick and threw it in the waste basket under my dressing table. For that time of the morning, everything looked as perfect as it was going to; adding a ballgown would be suspicious. Instead, I wore white linen trousers that were transparent in the right lighting, and a thin-strapped black top that was tight enough to show the curve of me. It would look good later, too, when Fin came home and found me passed out on the sofa – staged, on the pretence of waiting for him like the doting wife he wanted but wouldn't ask for.

'Knock, knock,' I said as I tapped the open front door.

'Come in, hon,' Nicole shouted from down a winding

corridor. I reasoned they were in the kitchen, so I closed the door behind me and walked through. 'Look at you,' she said, as soon as I stepped into the space. The reaction was so quick that I thought she must have had it ready, regardless of how I'd looked. I'd try a cloth sack for the next visit to see whether the effect was the same. 'You always look like you've strolled in from somewhere glamorous.'

'She does, doesn't she?' Xara spoke around a mouthful of biscuit. The room wreaked of sugar and sentiment.

'Coffee in the pot, hon, help yourself. Xara is telling me what a shit Derm is.'

She sighed. 'I didn't say he was being a shit.'

'You've started without me.' I took a seat at the table for four. I wondered whether Nicole had still believed Eliah wanted children when they bought this set together. 'Do I need a CliffsNotes or is it easy to catch up on as you go?'

'Don't you think Xara deserves a holiday?'

From what? 'I mean, yes, but do you need to *deserve* a holiday to take one?'

Xara laughed. 'Agnes, you are *so* right. But would you try to tell my husband?'

'Dermot thinks they should be saving.' Nicole nudged a plate of oaty biscuits towards me. 'Help yourself, hon. I made so many. You know what I'm like.'

'What should you be saving for?' I looked back to Xara and ignored the offer of food. Nicole was the sort of pretty girl who wanted to sabotage other pretty girls. She did it with food, now, but since we'd moved in across the road from her, I'd had a clear image of her as the teenager who replaced the popular girl's spot-cream with grout when no one was looking.

The pair shared a look before Xara admitted, 'We're trying.'

'I see.' I sipped my coffee and swallowed the reaction: *Then he's right. You should be saving.* 'In which case, could you not argue that actually having some time away to connect and share some intimacy would be good for you both? And therefore conducive to a mini one being conceived.' It had only been eight months since we'd moved to the village but already I knew where my allegiances were meant to lie when it came to disagreements between husbands and wives. Besides that, three years of marriage had taught me everything I needed to know when it came to holidays, nights out with friends, and a cavalcade of other events that Fin had tried to police at one time or another. I smiled at them both. 'Can't hurt, can it?'

'It's super hard now you're trying, though, because you can't even play the sex card.' Nicole laughed as she spoke then looked at me. 'Do you know what I mean?'

No. I shook my head and flashed a clueless glance. We weren't big on orgasm denial in the Villin household unless the rules were pre-agreed. But something told me Nicole had a different technique in mind.

'Agnes and Fin are too happy to know about that.' Xara joined the joke. 'Nic reckons that if you withhold sex for long enough, your husband will eventually just give in to whatever you want.'

'Interesting.' I sipped from my mug again to hide my reaction. *Problem one: blackmail and emotional abuse. Problem two: the assumption that women don't like sex as much as–* 'It seems counterintuitive to getting pregnant, Nicole is right,' I added, and said nothing of the wrongness of the plan.

'I think I'll talk to him about it all again when he gets home.'

'So we can expect another front lawn show?' Nicole asked.

Xara gently kicked her under the table. 'One time.'

'One time was enough,' I joined the joke. 'I nearly missed a benefit for that.'

Nicole groaned. 'Another work event?'

'What can I say, the higher Fin gets up the ranks, the more

work events there look to be. He's worked hard for it all, though, and I knew it was part of the deal when we started out.' I held a neutral tone while I told the lie; it was such a familiar untruth by now. 'Besides, Dermot and Eliah both do their fair share of late nights at the office.'

'With fewer glitzy benefits, though,' Nicole complained.

'Oh, Nic. The next time I get called for one, how about you go for me?'

She huffed a laugh. 'And what, you'll stay with Eliah for the night?'

Perfect. 'I didn't have you down as a swapper.'

She slapped my arm. 'Agnes, you're terrible. Anyone want a refill?' She grabbed our empty cups as she spoke. 'And for the love of God, eat some of those cookies, will you? I've got a fundraiser that I'm making meals for this evening and I need this kitchen cleared before the afternoon arrives.'

Xara reached for a third biscuit and said, 'We'd better leave some for Eliah.'

'He can have my share,' I said as I took the handle on the fresh cup Nicole offered. Refilled and piping hot, which meant I didn't have a sip to hide behind. 'You know what I'm like, too much sugar and my IBS will jump up to the thatched roof and have a fine old time. Eli will enjoy them more than me.' I saw Nicole shoot me a quizzical look so I corrected myself, 'Sorry, Eliah. Force of habit from Fin.'

She made a noise of agreement, then, and sat down with her own fresh drink. 'I've actually told him that I think we should look to do a bit of a health-kick, before the big cruise next year. Sorry, Xara,' she added the last part as an afterthought, in such a throwaway tone that anyone in earshot would guess that she wasn't *quite* sorry. 'We don't want to be at our worst when the pictures are taken on holiday, do we?'

I reached under the table to squeeze her thigh. 'I wouldn't call that anyone's worst. Eliah isn't in terrible shape either.'

'God, that's just how you want your husband described, isn't it?' she answered, and we all laughed. 'No, I'll take *good* shape over *not terrible* any day of the week. He actually said he might go to the gym tonight, which I thought was a good sign.'

I smiled behind my cup. 'Maybe he'll see Fin there.'

'Is he on a health-kick, too?' Xara asked.

I shook my head. *No, he's just looking for a beard for while he fucks a colleague.* 'He's stressed, I think, and it helps him so much to burn off energy there. Everything is fine and dandy, but still, he'll be like a new man tomorrow. It's best to give him space when he's this wound up as well.' But then I revised the comment. 'Not that he's nasty, only... uptight.'

Nicole nodded like she understood. 'Eliah gets exactly the same. Maybe he'll find something similar in the gym.' She laughed as she spoke, though, then added, 'Or the fridge when I'm not looking. Either-or.'

'I'm sure he'll find something that helps him one of these days,' I agreed.

'How about video games? I know it sounds stupid, but I swear, some nights, Dermot just needs to smash the hell out of something on his laptop screen and then after that it's like he's cleansed or something.'

'God, they never grow up, do they?' I joined, but Nicole was shaking her head.

'Eliah isn't the type for violence like that, not really.'

I blinked away the memory of my hand around his throat and said, 'No, well. Some people aren't.'

CHAPTER THREE

I'd always thought it was an unbecoming pastime: to sit at home and wait for a man. I remembered Mum doing it too often for my liking – though she made sure the tables eventually turned. It was past 6pm and the village was uncomfortably quiet. I missed the spit and churn of the city, and I resented Fin's exposure to it. There were times when the car would come home covered in the soot of commercial buildings; Fin's clothes would stink of second-hand civic fumes and I would inhale them deeply as though smelling another woman's perfume before I hung them back in his wardrobe. Now, I found I was eyeing the road, waiting for the blink of headlights to signal a homecoming.

The window seat in our living room was my lofty perch, with netted curtains to shield me while I looked out; a caged bird, I'd once joked with Fin, and he hadn't even smiled. From here, I could see Dermot and Xara in their living room; their stares glued to an out-of-sight television, his arm tucked around her in a comforting gesture. *Is that the picture of domestic bliss, now?* I wondered. I judged them harshly but there I was, alone in a house that my husband paid the mortgage for, waiting for a car to come tumbling down the road. *What position am I in to judge their closeness?*

I rested a hand around my neck and pressed the tenderness of an old bruise.

'Closeness comes in different forms, though,' I said to no one and my phone dinged as though in response.

Running late. So sorry. Will be there soon. xo

I sighed and threw the handset with a force. But the cushioned seat stopped it from making much of an impact. I thought of throwing the wine glass next to me for the sake of ruining something, but the clear-up wouldn't be worth it.

'Calm your shit, you silly woman.'

I reached for the phone and thumbed into social media. There were times when I was desperate for Fin to make a mistake, although I'd never been sure of what I thought might come of it. I clicked into his profile and scrolled for new updates. *Has someone tagged you somewhere, love?* I wouldn't leave him; I knew that much. Not that he'd be clumsy enough to give me a reason to. There, glaring in the brilliant light of his tailored profile, was a check-in to the university from earlier in the day, and a check-in to the gym from only twenty minutes earlier. I huffed: *How close must he have been parked for the check-in to reach?* I hit 'like' to let him know the effort hadn't gone unnoticed and then clicked back into the search bar. Facebook knew me too well; there Nicole was, right at the top of the suggestions.

She was a whore for the limelight. The fundraiser she'd donated meals to was actually a party put together in aid of raising money for Undernourished: a caring-for-creatures programme developed to help stray animals outside of the UK find a home within it. Although why rich people felt the need to throw a party to mark these things was always beyond me. It always seemed more time efficient to donate the money spent on the party, and take a night off from being a trophy. *But what do I know?*

Nicole's timeline was packed with pictures of filter-effect platters that she'd put together for the occasion: goat's cheese and cranberry tarts; meat skewers; crisp prawns with home-made dips. She had staple items that she rolled out: things she made well, but things that photographed well, too. After the first 'open house' where *all* the neighbours were encouraged together to socialise, I realised Nicole was a woman who played to her strengths – at least when it came to impressing other people.

In answer to the age-old question, 'Oh, but what does she do all day?' Nicole would be on-hand and ready with a gluten-free menu with dairy-free options on the side – and a photo diary of the lot, in case anyone cared to view it. Her Instagram was the amateur cook's equivalent of the enthusiasm shown by actual mothers when it came to photographing their children. Sans offspring, Nicole took pictures of tartlets instead.

That night, her Facebook looked similar. Although the string of images was broken up with one of her standing in between two old boys, their smiles wide and Nicole's tight-lipped. She's insecure about her smile, Eliah had dropped out once before slamming his hand tight across his mouth, as though he'd let out a trade secret that might fuel housewife warfare. She'd been tagged in this picture, captioned: 'Blessed to have this angel among us this evening. What a feast! Thank you, Nicole.'

'I bet she fucking loves that.' I scrolled further down and saw yet more pictures of food, these ones slightly messier. Other people had uploaded their plates and tagged Nicole; her name stitched into pastry, prosciutto and empty plates. 'She'll love that, too.'

It wasn't worth checking Xara's profile. Her and Dermot were still huddled together in low lighting across the road. I craned around to catch sight of Jessa and Umi's home but there was no sign of life there, either, and it crossed my mind that our token lesbians might be at the fundraiser with Nicole. They were known for their good deeds. But before I had time to pull up their profiles a set of headlights flickered at the end of the road: one flash, then two. After the second they stayed on, and he drove the stretch down into our circle of homes.

It would take a minute, still, for him to get sorted. So I stretched and moved to the kitchen, poured a second glass of white for me and a splash of red for him. He wouldn't want too much; he never did. I heard the back door – knock-knock, a pause, then, knock-knock-knock – and when I didn't answer he let himself in, as was customary. He looked dishevelled, shattered from a day at the office I guessed. I held back a sigh. *He's going to want to be soft.* Eliah hadn't been my first choice but Dermot wouldn't be swayed, and I reasoned a man with that much determination wouldn't let me do what I'd wanted anyway.

'You took your time.' I handed him a glass.

He only took enough to wet his lips and then handed it back to me. 'Long day.'

'Rain check?'

'Are you mad?' He closed the distance between us and I felt a hand pinch either side of my waist; I imagined him sizing me up for something. 'Nicole will be out for hours yet.'

'Fin won't be. Here?' I nodded to the island behind me. If I could keep him out of the bedroom, there was a chance I could keep the softness out of him, too. When he didn't answer, I leaned forward to kiss from jawline to ear before I set my palm on the Adam's apple bulge of his throat. 'Please?'

Unprompted, he lifted me first, then started to unbutton his shirt.

Everyone has their buzzwords.

When Fin found me I was huddled under the soft furnishings of the living room; blankets reserved for looking good, for guests, or holding me warm on the nights when my husband wasn't home. I'd showered and redressed after Eliah slipped out; reapplied make-up from where I'd sweated it off and swilled my hair free from the smell of someone else's aftershave. I hadn't felt tired when I arranged myself in the lounge but I must have been because the front door woke me, shortly followed by Fin's face lowered into my watercolour vision.

'Sweetheart, you didn't need to wait up.'

I made a show of stretching accompanied by cushy noises that he'd approve of. 'I must have drifted. What time is it? Is it quite late?'

He brushed my fringe from my face. 'Late enough for bed. Come on.' He pressed a kiss against my forehead, then, and I inhaled the smell from his collar, smiled: *He wasn't wearing that shirt this morning.* 'I'll carry you.'

It was such a rehearsed routine that I hardly needed an instruction. I wrapped my arms around his neck while he tucked an arm beneath my knees; when I leaned towards him he wrapped his other arm around me and lifted. Like a meek one, I even rested my head on his shoulder for the journey from downstairs to up. He kicked open the bedroom door and I sighed at the gesture. We were a fairy tale in many ways, cautionary in others. He lowered me onto the bed and kissed my forehead again before he moved away. The room stayed dark apart from a throw of light that came in from the bathroom shortly after Fin disappeared in there. I heard the splash of cold water; brushing of teeth; urine colliding with porcelain. But I didn't hear the click or hum of the shower heating which explained the clean shirt, too.

It was minutes later when he curled around me. 'Tell me about your day.'

'I played with the other domesticated wild cats.'

He huffed a laugh and the heat of his breath landed on my shoulder. 'Agnes, you shouldn't talk about your friends like that.'

'I never would.'

'Oh hush, you like them really.' He kissed my shoulder blade. 'How are they?'

'Nicole was trying to feed us carbohydrates while we made a witches brew of ideas for how Xara might trick Dermot into taking her on holiday.'

'I'm surprised Dermot doesn't want a break, the way he's been working.'

'No.' I pressed my face into the pillow and spoke into the feathers, 'He wants to save instead, apparently, work on getting money put by for the future.'

I didn't tell him why, though. I didn't want to risk putting thoughts in his head.

CHAPTER FOUR

It was days later when I noticed. Fin stood tall behind me while I was seated at my dressing table, stretching the skin of my neck this way and that.

'You should have knocked if it was too much.'

I'd never knocked, and likely never would. There was something else in him when he bore down like that, and I'd always guessed that leaving him unfulfilled would be more dangerous than not.

'It's fine, it'll cover.' I reached for my foundation. 'I'll blend.'

'What if the doctor–'

'The doctor won't,' I interrupted him.

'And you don't want me there today?'

I locked eyes with him through the mirror. 'It's not worth the annual leave.'

Fin leaned forward to kiss the crown of my head. 'I love you.'

'I love you.' I was already busying myself with make-up sponges. 'Go, you'll be late for work. Are you home at the normal time this evening?' I tried to keep suspicion out of my voice – like a good and trusting housewife.

'All being well. Text me to let me know how you get on.'

I only grumbled in response. I was too busy trying to colour-match my bruising to the natural skin tones hidden deep underneath.

———

There were thirty-four tiles on the ceiling of the waiting room. There had been that many for the last two years; bar one month when a workman had broken through a tile to get to a hidden electrical box. But it had been fixed by the following appointment. There were still thirty-four tiles, but I counted them five times because my doctor was running late. I huffed loud enough to catch the receptionist's attention and then checked my watch, huffed again. She only flashed me a raised eyebrow and went back to her paper-pushing without an explanation.

Minutes later, while I was mid-scroll on Eliah's Facebook page, someone pulled my attention away. 'Agnes?'

'Dr Neilson.' I flashed a tight smile and stood. 'I was deep in sleuthing,' I joked.

He laughed and said, 'Social media makes detectives of us all. I'm sorry for running so late. Shall we?' He gestured to his open doorway and I walked in ahead of him. I knew the room layout by now. It was muscle memory to walk in, take a seat in the visitor's chair; always the left, leaving the right empty for a husband who didn't come with me. By request, not that anyone else was to know. 'How are you feeling?'

I looked around as I answered, 'Hormonal.'

'Yes, well.' He opened a side drawer and pulled out my file. 'That fits the bill.'

Dr Neilson had become our doctor by referral. 'The best in the business,' my GP had said. 'If he can't get you pregnant then no one will.' Fin and I had laughed in response but I thought I was the only one of us who'd found the phrasing sincerely amusing. Fin didn't like the challenge it posed. We'd been twenty minutes into the car journey home when he'd suggested that we source a female consultant. Bitter from the pills and the prodding and the poking, I'd asked whether that was a suggestion for my comfort or his. In matters of the uterus, he allowed me to go unchallenged. It was one of the few areas where such a luxury was afforded. After the first handful of appointments, though, I'd practically imprinted on the good doctor who made jokes and shed light and said nothing judgemental of my inability to produce an heir.

Unlike Fin.

I knew children had been important to him. During our third dalliance he'd lifted my legs onto his shoulders as though checking my form. In the years since, our – *my* – lack of natural conception had started to make me feel like a disingenuous sales assistant who'd sold a faulty product. When the tests had shown nothing wrong – with neither him *nor* me – I'd suggested alternatives: adoption; surrogacy. Fin had only shaken his head and said, 'Maybe you're just not meant to be a mother.'

'Everything still looks normal here,' Neilson said. It pulled me out of the memories. 'How are your periods?'

'Regular, still. Clockwork, in fact.'

'Spotting?'

'None.'

'Abdominal discomfort?'

'Minimal, and only in the days before my period.'

He licked his finger and skimmed a page. 'Shall we get that smear done while you're here today?'

'Ooh.' I used a girlish tone. 'Please, doctor.'

Neilson had good humour enough to laugh. 'I know, it's not my favourite job either.'

'Is that meant to make me feel better, doc?' I shrugged my jacket off.

He looked up in the air as though searching for an answer. 'I really don't know.'

In the minutes after, Dr Neilson averted his eyes while I slipped free of my underwear. The man had been inside me so many times that a modesty sheet hardly seemed worth it anymore. Still, he handed me a paper-blanket to cover myself with before asking me to lie back – 'Legs bent, Agnes, if you please, feet together and knees apart.' – like I didn't already know the routine. The jokes fell away, then, and I counted the ceiling tiles while he quietly unwrapped equipment. On average, Neilson took one hundred and ninety-two seconds to soft brush my cervix but he was running ahead of time that day.

'All done.' He pulled the speculum free in a swift movement and my breath caught in my throat. 'Apologies, Agnes, should've–'

'Agreed on a safe word,' I interrupted and he spluttered a laugh; a surprised one, as though the comment had caught him off-guard. 'You're all right, doc. It's not like I didn't know you were pulling out.'

'By all means use the sheet to... Well, you know. I'll pull the curtain closed.'

I wiped myself clean of lubricant and let my dress fall back around my knees.

'You'll write with the results?' I asked as I pushed the covering back. I crossed to my seat and grabbed my jacket without sitting. 'Two weeks?'

'I'm sure that'll be the case. As always–'

'If there's a need for a colposcopy we'll call,' I parroted in a deliberately masculine voice.

'It's almost like you don't need me.' He flashed me a sad kind of smile and I saw the sympathy come off him in wiggly, cartoon waves. 'Agnes, I know you're hoping that things will change, or will have changed, during one of these visits. But there really is no reason why, or no *medical* reason why this isn't happening for you. I can't imagine how hard that must be to hear, especially for your husband, too.'

At the mention of Fin my hand went to my throat in an automatic gesture. I fingered the bruising; it was deep under foundation but with the right pressure it was easy to find.

'I wouldn't discourage you from trying, of course, and I realise you've entertained the possibility of adoption already, which has been dismissed?' He paused for confirmation.

I pressed at the side of my neck and made a noise of agreement.

'But I do wonder at what this might be doing to your marriage, and your general well-being, too, of course.'

I smiled. *Interesting order there, doc.* 'My husband and I are fine.'

'You've been coming to these appointments alone for some months now.'

'I told Fin it isn't worth wasting the holiday.' I draped my jacket around my shoulders. 'And no, nothing is changing so there really is little use in the appointments. Apart from setting mine and my husband's minds at ease that there's nothing more we can be doing, beyond having sex like teenagers.'

Neilson chuckled. 'Well at least you can be thankful for that, surely.'

'There are worse things.' I made for the exit. 'It's been a pleasure, as always.'

'I'll write to you.'

'Oh, that's what they all say...' I was halfway out the door already.

The world outside was painfully bright and I was glad to be blindsided by something other than my body. Fin had texted once – 'Don't forget to let me know how you get on.' – and Eliah twice: 'I miss you xo' and 'Are you free today? xo'.

For half an hour I rolled around replies to both. One of the perks to Dr Neilson was the positioning of his office; right in the centre of the designer district, within catching distance of the Yummy Mummy club members who spent their days charging happiness to their husband's credit cards. I blew out my judgement in a long, slow breath; *aren't you one of them, after all?*

It would take more than a handbag, though, so when I was back in the car I replied to Fin to report no changes. Then I texted Eliah: 'Tell me where to be' followed by a single kiss.

BEFORE

He pushed himself upright in bed and winced. There were nicks and grazes all down his torso, small war wounds on the skin. But it was the taut wax that made me wince for him. In the time since I'd let it run from the well of a lit candle, it had landed, splashed and hardened so his torso looked like a crayon rendition of a Pollock portrait. If I were to fence his body in with broad planks of wood, I could sell this sex as art. Though as he picked and rubbed and–

'Fuck, that's definitely got some hair.'

I wasn't sure he'd appreciate me making him into a masterpiece.

'Why do you like it so much?' I propped myself up on my elbow and set a hand over his, to pause him from peeling at himself. He shook me free, though, and carried on with the job at hand. 'Doesn't it hurt you?'

He smiled. 'Did you ever think that's *why* I like it so much?'

'That makes no sense to me.' I flipped over to my front and rested my head on a cold patch of pillow. His sheets were crisp white whenever I came over and I was always conscious of leaving make-up behind; though it would at least make it harder

27

for him to bring another woman in once he'd shipped me out – unless he went to the hassle of changing the sheets, that is. I shook the thought free and closed my eyes. It wasn't attractive to be jealous in this situation; he'd already told me as much.

'What are you thinking?' he asked when I'd been silent for too long.

'Nothing.'

'That's a lie.'

I half-laughed. 'You don't know that.'

'Of course I do, Agnes. It's one of the things I like most; you're never still.'

'It's one of the things I like least.'

He fidgeted until he was lower down the bed, his head level with my own. 'Seriously, what are you thinking about? The wax?' I opened my eyes in time to catch him brushing away crumbs of candle from his stomach. It was the third time we'd done this, and I knew there was more to come. But I was still adjusting to the freehand at hurting someone; still waiting for the glass floor to crack and for me to find there was a catch. 'You know the deal,' he turned to look at me, 'if you're ever uncomfortable use–'

'I know the deal,' I cut him off.

'So, if it's not that, then...'

'How many women do you let dribble hot wax over you?' A laugh chased the question out. 'Christ, what a thing to ask the person you're sleeping with.'

'You're not sleeping with me.' He leaned forward and kissed my forehead, then spoke in a lower voice, 'But you are my favourite little young thing, Agnes. My absolute favourite of them all.'

CHAPTER FIVE

I t left a bad taste in my mouth to sleep with the husband and then pay the wife. But at least with Nicole-as-caterer I knew the services I was getting – and what she expected in return. She referred to her low fees as 'friends with benefits' but she said it without a hint of flirtation so I tried to swallow down the urge for a joke. Of course, an unwritten part of my invoice for Nicole, scribbled somewhere in invisible ink, was that I stayed with her in the kitchen throughout the proceedings. It was a Saturday afternoon and Fin was working in his upstairs office; a paper with a deadline, that was as much as I knew. Meanwhile, Nicole filled the room with Cardi B – a music choice that absolutely didn't suit her middle-class, plum-in-the-proverbial upbringing – and asked about our plans for the summer months.

'When Fin takes time off from work, I mean.'

I watched her grate a carrot; pulling the blade back toward her one hand while forcing it away again with the other. It took a true effort to look away.

'I'm not sure he ever takes time off work.' I flashed a tight smile. 'But you know all about that, don't you? It's part of the housewife creed that we let them earn the money, so that we might spend the money, and we make no complaint.' I cocked an eyebrow; I hoped she'd challenge it.

'Well.' She gestured at the ingredients spread out across the island. 'Actually...'

Atta girl.

'I know it's only pocket money, but the catering stuff really is very fulfilling. I'm giving people...' She paused and bunched her arms towards her chest, screwed her face up with a smile and sniffed hard, as though she might inhale the right word from the work surface. 'Nourishment. Is that the word I'm looking for?' She went back to grating, then, but didn't wait for an actual answer. 'I know it might not seem very important but look, take this meal we're making, for example. What's the occasion?'

Parole officer visit. 'Fin's parents are coming.'

'Perfect.' Scrape. 'Fin's parents are coming. You'll all sit around the table together...' Scrape. 'And you'll eat dinner, laugh and joke...' Scrape. 'Maybe name-drop the caterer...' Scrape. 'The whole afternoon will revolve around you having dinner together and– Bugger!'

She caught my attention. 'Are you okay?'

'Do you have a first aid kit?' She raised her finger to her mouth and sucked.

'Of course.' I hopped off the stool and crossed to the cupboard behind her. The green box was buried at the back and I had to move three tubes of arnica to free it. 'Here, let me see?' I said when I was alongside her at the counter.

'Does someone bruise easily?'

'Me,' I answered without looking up. The cut on her finger was a small one; a papercut would have done worse. Still, I guided it under the cold tap to ease the bleeding and asked her to stay there while the water ran. 'I've got some antiseptic plasters somewhere, for over the end of...' I faded out when I heard the footfalls, though.

'If we wanted blood in the food, Agnes would do the cooking herself,' Fin said as he rounded the corner. He leaned on the island that separated us from him and winked at me. 'Everything okay in here?'

'Only me being clumsy.' Nicole waved the bandaged finger at him while I packed the kit away. I looked up in time to catch her cheeks change colour. *Hm.* 'I was so busy talking about the beauty of cooking that I forgot about the dangers of it.' She laughed and then picked up the grater. 'How are you, Finian?'

'Fin, please,' he corrected her, not for the first time. 'Fit and well, though, Nicole, and yourself? Eliah?'

I slammed the cupboard closed and crossed back to my seat. I missed her answer.

'Honestly, you two,' she said, when I came to a stop alongside Fin. He smiled and wrapped an arm around me; he'd likely guessed what was coming. 'Every time I see the pair of you I feel like laying down a red carpet. Even on a rainy Saturday at home you're both bloody gorgeous.'

'Come now, Eliah and you are a good-looking couple, aren't they, Fin?'

He squeezed me. 'Second best in the village, I'd say.'

'Fin!' I tapped his side and Nicole playfully tossed carrot peel at him. And for a moment or two things were blissfully normal. 'How's work?' I craned around to look up at him. 'Paper coming along nicely?'

'Funny you should ask.' He let me go, then, and went to the fridge to pull out water. He addressed only me, skirted around Nicole as though she'd been erased from the room and I wondered whether it made her feel like the help – or whether she was into being ignored by husbands. 'I've just had another abstract accepted. There's a conference happening in Boston later in the year and they're especially interested in the work we've just put through under that bid. Fancy a little trip?'

'Oh, yes please,' Nicole said under her breath and we both ignored her.

'I'll check my diary.' I cocked an eyebrow, smirked. 'Of course I fancy a trip.'

'Good.' He gave me a kiss on the cheek as he passed. 'It'll likely be Christmas.'

Fin had far more reasons to stay at home at Christmas than I did. If he was happy to leave his family behind for the holiday season, then I wasn't going to argue. It had never been a special enough time of year for me to mind who I spent it with, or where.

'You're so lucky,' Nicole said when Fin was climbing the stairs again. 'Handsome husband, dream home, little trips.'

I laughed. 'What's so different about us, Nic?' There was a long pause where she concentrated too much on skinning a small potato. 'Hey, is everything okay at home?' There was an interest in me that I was trying desperately to swallow back down into my belly. 'We can talk, if there's something going on?'

'There's nothing. There really is nothing. But...' She leaned in and lowered her voice. 'Honestly, Agnes, do you ever think of just leaving?' She pulled back and robbed me of the chance to answer again. 'Stupid question, why would you? You and your husband like each other *all* the time, *never* a cross word.' She sounded severely put out by her perceptions of us but I wasn't about to correct them; I only flashed an awkward smile. 'I'm sorry, I'm not– God, it sounds like I'm envious about you being happy, which I'm absolutely not. I just – especially lately, this is... I just feel like Eliah and I aren't as *connected* as we used to be.'

A gulp echoed up from me. 'Sexually?'

She laughed, then, and said, 'Always straight to the point with you.'

'Well, I'm paying you by the hour.' I winked and reached across to squeeze her hand. 'You can trust me, Nicole.'

Another long pause followed where I imagined her weighing up what she could and couldn't share. 'Christ, here I am talking about connection like it's a two-way problem and it bloody isn't.' She dropped her utensil and vegetable at once, pushed her hand through her hair and I imagined the smells she must have left behind. 'I can trust you,' she said, but I knew it was a question.

I used my best doe eyes and nodded.

'Agnes, I think – God, I think the reason Eliah and I aren't connecting is because I might have feelings for someone else.' Then, hurriedly, as though snatching away the option of changing her mind, she added, 'I kissed someone. I kissed someone else.'

I tried very hard not to smile.

I love it when people surprise me...

The kitchen looked lived in by the time she left. Nicole had peeled and chopped and soaked. There was a joint of something in a slow cooker that I didn't even know we owned, with strict instructions that it was to be left overnight. By every appliance there were further instructions still – 'Turn the hob to six for thirty minutes...' and 'Set the oven to 150 to heat this through...' – and even without having fully cooked the meal, somehow the room was vacuum-packed with smells.

I hadn't turned on the lights when I came down; there was

enough flooding in from the high moon. Fin was sleeping soundly upstairs but I was restless, bitten by an inability to close down for the night. So I tiptoed around the kitchen to set the kettle to boil, and wandered into the living room while I waited.

I pulled the soft throw from the sofa to drape around my shoulders before I went to the window. Every house was resting apart from one: Eliah and Nicole's bedroom window was lit. It wasn't mood lighting, though, but the yellow glare of an overhead bulb and it crossed my mind they might be a lights-on couple although I'd never had time to ask. Besides that, Eliah didn't like talking about Nicole when we were together. It wasn't for guilt, he'd once told me, only because he wanted to be efficient with time.

The kettle clicked to a full boil but I stayed rooted. Now I'd seen the light, I worried that I might miss something if I moved away. *Nicole, will you tell him, I wonder?* It crossed my mind that she might be telling him there and then, although I'd warned her not to. To start with, nothing good came from these confessions; to second, I knew she'd be disappointed with his answer. Eliah would either be (hypocritically) upset and instigate a split; or he wouldn't care at all.

'Those are my options?' she'd asked.

'That, or staying quiet.'

I heard the groan of a joist overhead. 'Do you want tea?' I asked when Fin was a few steps down. My stare was still fixed outside. There was a shadow in the curtain now; Eliah's silhouette, as though he were supporting himself on the windowsill. Fin came to a stop behind me, wrapped his arms around my middle where a baby bump would be. *Should be.* 'I couldn't drop off.'

'So you thought you'd spy on the neighbours?'

'It's better than television.'

He craned around and kissed my temple. 'Are they arguing?'

'Too soon to tell.'

'In which case I'll make us both a cup. If the light is out by the time it's brewed, we'll go back to bed. Decaf for you?' he asked, then left the room without my order. By now Fin knew I'd take what I was given.

CHAPTER SIX

Marina was the type of woman who, after giving birth, left the hospital unblemished. I had always imagined her suited in baby blue with a skirt at a suitable length – just below the knee, that is – with a small Finian swaddled in blankets, no doubt hand-stitched by blind nuns. She was also the woman Fin wanted me to be when I grew up. Toby – Tobias, in formal settings, but Toby when he was visiting us – beeped the horn twice when they arrived.

When I made it to the front door, Marina was standing at the end of our cobbled walkway, as though waiting for a carpet to be laid out. Fin squeezed past me – 'Agnes, come on' – and went to meet her. He kissed her cheek, took her hand and led her toward the open doorway, and she cooed a thank you that made it seem like she never would have made it alone. I stepped aside to let them in, but I was hardly through my own greeting when Fin ushered her into the lounge – where she would sit on the soft furnishing reserved for royalty.

'Agnes.' Toby rolled his eyes in a playful way. I'd always been better with fathers.

'Toby, so glad you could make it. Come on in.'

I shut the door behind us. After a glance around the hallway, he turned. 'I assume her lady is being tended to by her aide for the afternoon. Does that make you mine or should I source booze myself?'

I laughed. 'I'm sure if we tap the fridge, a crisp white will come rushing out.' I took him by the arm and steered him into the kitchen where food was cooking at a low hum. 'Will Marina have white?'

'She's driving us home so it'd better be–'

'Soda water with a twist of lime?'

He winked at me. 'Aren't you a good one?'

There was a set of flashcards in my bedside table. During my sleepless night, I'd decided to make good use of the time and brush up on my studies. There were key facts hastily scribbled in Fin's handwriting. The ink was tired now, after four years of wear, but the information hadn't changed much. There was the occasional amendment – Marina was vegetarian for about five minutes which led to an annotation and then, later, a strikethrough – but largely they were a couple who had long ago decided on their roles. Not dissimilar to me and their son.

'You're putting on a good show today,' Toby said, and I was glad my reaction was shielded by the fridge. I was out of sight long enough for him to add, 'This looks like a feast for fifty people. Is it just us?'

When I closed the door I saw that he was checking the dining table for signs of life: only four settings.

'It is. You know me, I'm terrible with these things.' *Which isn't a lie.* 'Say when?' I held the edge of the wine bottle over the rim of a glass. After two inches I laughed and stopped. 'Marina will tell you it's unbecoming to have more than that in one sitting.'

'Quite right.' He reached across the island, snatched the

glass and downed the contents in one hideous gulp. 'There, top it up would you, Agnes?'

I raised an eyebrow. 'You're the boss.'

Toby chuckled, paused, and then said, 'Yes, I suppose I am.' There was a smugness to him that I recognised from his son. *Oh, to be a middle-class white male*, I thought as I topped up my glass with one inch of white to be sociable, and then Fin's with two inches of red. I knew my limits even if men didn't. 'He's still drinking that?'

'He thinks it's classier than white.' I passed across a tall drink for Marina. There was already condensation dripping down the glass and I had to resist the urge to grab a tea towel. Instead, I imagined Marina's disapproval at pulling away with a wet hand. 'Join them. I'll follow in a second, I just want to check how everything is coming along in here.'

'Yes, chef.'

Toby disappeared into the living room. Only seconds later, though, Fin appeared to take his father's place in the kitchen. He stared hard at me, twitched his head, like a predator spotting movement, then snatched his glass from the counter. I hadn't realised how hard I'd been gripping the edge of the work surface until cramp ran through my fingers. For the first time in my short life, I was grateful for the squeal of the oven timer.

There was a chorus of appreciative noises around the table. Marina had complimented my cooking no less than *three* times, and every time I felt my stomach gripped by acid nerves that Fin might bat her kindness away with the truth. Things continued to go well though, even when fertility was mentioned – 'We haven't given up just yet.' Fin squeezed my leg beneath the table – and eventually work. 'Agnes might go back, it all depends, doesn't it?' he answered for me, when Toby had asked about my plans. But the lack of a child *and* the lack of a career looked to be too much of a cross for one mother-in-law to bear.

'We could always get a puppy,' I joked.

Fin remained stone-faced. 'I don't think that's a good idea.'

'You loved having Rover around when you were a child,' Toby added in support.

'But now I'm an adult, and there isn't a child here.'

In the seconds after, we fell back into soft noises of enjoyment; like dogs kicking leaves over the worst of their business. Marina was soon pushing a small family of roast potatoes around her plate and I wondered whether the carbohydrates were the problem or whether there was something brewing.

'If you're full, you can leave it, Mum. Agnes won't be offended. Will you?'

'Of course not. There was so much choice, after all.'

'Well, there's no chance of me leaving any.' Toby reached his fork to his wife's plate and speared the hardened skin of a roaster. 'Duck fat, was it, Agnes?'

I hesitated too long and Marina noticed it; I was sure. 'Yes, from memory. Although there was a lot going on in here yesterday.' I laughed; the fine-tuned laugh that I'd tailored during my first meeting with Marina and Toby some years ago. It was so distinct, so to-the-taste of their social circle, and I had to keep it up whenever we were with them now and I was expected to be amused. 'I wouldn't be at all surprised if something else had been thrown into the mix by accident.'

'Hm.' Marina pushed her plate away. 'That sounds very creative.'

Hm. That sounds like a carefully spoken criticism. 'I get like that in the kitchen.' *Ask your son*, I wanted to add, thinking of the island: the smash of a serving dish and splattered cheese sauce that decorated the floor only hours before their arrival.

'Anyway, Agnes, we've talked, talked, talked. How's your family?'

Even Toby stopped chewing.

'Mum, I've told you, Agnes and her mum aren't speaking at the moment.'

'Still?' It was directed at me, but Fin answered.

'Still.'

She looked affronted, as though she were the one who'd been phased out. 'And your father, Agnes, how's he doing? Assuming you–'

'Mum!'

Marina looked shocked at his tone. But it wasn't an unfamiliar one to me. I slipped a hand under the shield of the table and kneaded at the soft flesh of his thigh. There was a flicker of tension there, the tightening and loosening of muscles like trying to keep something clenched. He set his hand over the top of my own, then, and shot me a hooded glance. I only nodded and turned back to his mother.

'Dad actually passed away, Marina, some months ago now.'

'Fin– Finian, you didn't mention.' She spoke to him but was fixed to me.

'No, well, it's Agnes' business, isn't it?' He leaned over and laid a soft kiss on my cheek, then collected his cutlery and scored into the last slice of meat on his plate. The puncture of it made me queasy. 'Some things aren't for sharing.'

Toby cleared his throat with an abrupt cough. 'Agnes, we're both terribly sorry to hear this. Aren't we, Marina?'

'It goes without saying.'

'But I'm saying it anyway,' he snapped and side-eyed her.

'Thank you, Toby, that's kind of you to say.' I could see that she was itching to know; Marina made slight jerks in her seat as though being physically teased. 'It was cancer in the end, which is a terrible shame given the things they can do these days. But I'm told that they caught it quite late, so there was nothing to be done. He had a good life, for what it's worth.' I shook my head and forced the beginnings of tears; the slight glisten that comes with the loosening of ducts. 'I don't know why people say that, like it makes it better for someone to have... To have...'

'Sweetheart.' Fin tucked an arm around my back and pulled me to him. 'I think that's quite enough family talk for one day. Dad, would you and Mum mind clearing the plates away, please? If Mum's quite finished.' Though it was clear he wasn't talking about the food. I imagined the look he must have given her over my ducked head; the that's-the-wrong-dress look, or the why-didn't-you-laugh? 'I think I'll see Agnes to the living room if that's all right.' He leaned forward and kissed the back of my head, still pressed against him, and I nodded into his chest. 'We'll be back in a moment.'

Fin and I pushed back our seats together and left Toby and Marina to their servings of tension; the one part of dinner I hadn't needed Nicole for. On the journey to the living room, I kept my head drooped but when Fin set me on the sofa, and cosied in alongside me, he lifted my chin to get a look at my face. He pressed the edge of his index finger under my chin, his thumb pressed over it as though pinching me. I blinked hard to clear my eyes and then flashed a sad smile.

'She wasn't to know.'

'It isn't her business.' He kissed me square on the mouth, then, roughly, held my chin so I couldn't pull away from the pressure of him. 'I'll get rid of them early.'

'We still have dessert.'

'I can portion it into Tupperware.'

I set my palm flat against the side of his face then and felt the anger like something shifting under the skin. 'I'm fine for them to stay.' The kiss I gave him was a soft one; our lips barely touched but his breath was hot against me. 'Family is so important. Losing Mum and Dad has taught me that. You should make the most of these moments with them; we both should.' It occurred to me that I was talking about my mother as though she'd also passed, and I wondered whether it was a flicker of wishful thinking.

He opened up the space between us but looked hard into me. 'You are perfect.'

I only smiled and shifted my stare to the window. *You keep thinking that.*

CHAPTER SEVEN

Violet was my most outlandish friend: flirtatious; shameless; utterly gorgeous – and passionately hated by my husband. She hadn't visited the house since we'd moved in on account of her not being allowed to; not that Fin had encouraged me to share that excuse exactly. In the interest of keeping up appearances, I was to tell Violet that we weren't yet settled and perhaps she could visit when we were. Fin was willing to be branded as many unsavoury things, but he seemed to live in fear of anyone ever thinking of him as rude. 'Besides,' he'd said one morning, 'it gives you the chance to get out of the house if you travel to the city to see her.' So I did – at every opportunity I was given.

Vi and I had spent most of our post-grad years together. While I busied myself with a masters and the waste-of-a-degree that came after it, Vi was busy with a master's by research that eventually led to a doctorate in psychology. Rather than take the route into education, though, she went into practice. And now she boasted some of the most fucked-up private clients the city had to offer. She specialised in cases that shouldn't or couldn't see the light of day, and she valued that level of hush-hush.

On my jaunts into the city, I always let Vi choose where we'd meet. It was my sorry-for-being-a-distant-friend play; plus, she knew all the best places. I was twenty minutes late when I walked into Bacchus: an underground bar that took Google Maps plus four requests of help from total strangers to find.

She was sitting in a high-backed armchair with a waiter leaning over her. *So, she's used these twenty minutes wisely...* I smiled. She looked stunning. Her legs were crossed, highlighting the slit of her skirt that ran too high for daylight hours; the blouse was crisp white with a long floral trim around both sleeves and the collar; and her hair was braided, trailing down over her left shoulder to pool in her lap. The outfit was neat, tailored, Violet – but she would have looked this good in anything.

The waiter was, I thought, just about to try his luck with getting her number when I came to a stop by the table. 'Mind if I cut in?' I pulled his attention up and from the corner of my eye I saw Vi smirk. 'Thanks for keeping her warm for me.' I dropped into the matching armchair and shrugged my jacket free.

'She'll have what I'm having. Thanks, love.' She didn't even look at him as she spoke. *Poor kid doesn't know what's hit him.* 'You're late.'

'This place may as well be in the back of a child's wardrobe.' I glanced around the place then, to take in the candle-style wall fixtures, the swag and drape curtains. It looked like a space stripped from a Victorian novel and I wondered whether someone would appear with opium offerings at the same time as my drink arrived.

'I knew you'd like it here.'

My head snapped around and I caught Vi watching me. 'Simple things please–'

'You dare accuse yourself of having a simple mind.' She

cocked an eyebrow, and I flashed my hands palm up in surrender. 'How's life treating you?'

'Sorry to interrupt,' the waiter spoke to Vi even though he was setting a drink down for me. 'One Death in the Afternoon.' He turned then. 'Is there anything else I can get for either of you?'

'Keep those coming, would you, love? That'll be all.' She gestured, as though waving him away, and he followed instruction. 'He's a cute one, isn't he?'

'You'd eat him alive.' I leaned forward to inspect the drink. 'Death in the Afternoon? Are you taking the piss?'

'It's a Hemingway Champagne cocktail elsewhere. I thought you'd approve.'

'Because of the literary reference?'

'No, because of the absinthe.'

I shot back. 'That's too much for an afternoon drink in the city.'

'So stay over! What's there to rush back for?' Her smirk was hidden behind her glass but from her tone I knew it was there. 'Oh, wait, let me guess...'

'How's life treating *you*, Miss Hot-Shot?'

'Dr Hot-Shot, thank you, Dr Villin.' She sipped her drink, winced and set it back down on the table. Violet was one of few people to remember that my title outlasted my marriage vows, and it was one of many reasons why I loved her. 'Life is good. Clients are keeping me busy, although not *so* busy that I can't take an afternoon off to get drunk at a high-end bar with my best friend.' She shrugged. 'What more could a woman ask for? Now, your turn.'

'Life is less interesting, but fine. Fin is being kept busy at work. I'm trying to play with the other housewives without snapping...' I drifted out. *What more is there?*

'That's a nice scarf you're wearing.'

45

I thumbed the edge of the fabric: chiffon, a faded burgundy polka dot print to add a splash of something to an otherwise black outfit.

'It was a present from Fin.'

'The scarf, or what's underneath it?'

I cracked into a laugh. 'Both?'

'He's still doing it, then,' she said, disapprovingly, as though she hadn't done worse with men over the years. Violet was the only person I had ever – could ever – confide in about Fin's behaviours. She'd helped me to decide on the ground rules: safe gesture; glass of water; don't chase unconsciousness. But she – like me – had expected it to be something we tried once or twice and then discarded, like so many other things. It had been years now, though, and the bruising left behind could always be read like a catalogue of our marriage at the time of infliction. He was misusing it. And that was the only thing in the world I couldn't tell her.

'I enjoy him doing it.'

She narrowed her eyes. 'You enjoy him doing it, or you enjoy giving him permission to? You're a riddle-mystery in control tendencies, Agnes.'

'Oh, please. I thought this was a social call, I didn't realise I'd come to the city for an appointment.' I sipped my own drink then, simply to have something to do, and I donned a poker face while it burnt its way down my insides. 'Hemingway was a raging misogynist and highly overrated in the literary world, you know, I can't see why his drink recipes should be trusted.'

She spluttered a laugh. 'Because it'll get us high as teenagers?'

'Violet, are you trying to get me drunk?'

'Always.' She blew a kiss then said, 'But we haven't finished talking about your husband.'

I sighed. 'Honestly, Vi, things are fine. I *enjoy* Fin doing it, that's why I let him do it. You know how this works, where the control is. I knock and he stops.' I flashed a tight smile and I hoped she wouldn't notice that I'd just told a flaming lie. 'What more is there to discuss?'

She nodded, slowly, as though processing the information. 'May I see?' I touched my scarf in question and she murmured. 'No judgement, but I'm curious about what you're hiding. And I'm not asking as a professional, I'm asking as a friend who can only see you during secret meet-ups in the city, because your husband doesn't want me at your house.'

'Violet, that's not–'

She held her hand up to cut me off. 'Love, don't.'

Like unwrapping a neat present, I pulled one end of the scarf and let the fabric fall away in a single action. It landed in my lap and I shuffled forward, then, to close some of the distance between us. When Vi had a good viewpoint, I tipped my head back to expose pressure marks, polka dots of purple, blue and yellow that would have complicated my outfit if I'd left them bare. With my head tipped back, I felt like a young girl in a gory slasher film waiting for something to take her. But when Violet did touch me it was gentle; packed with concern. She traced around each bruise as though my skin were braille, etched with the truth of how the marks got there. The concentration on her face reminded me of all the times I read essays aloud to her, only to be met with a set stare and her stock response of, 'It's all just pretty language and theory to me.' I felt a hard exhale land on my skin and I flinched.

'I'm sorry.' She moved away, dropped back against the tall seat. 'It looks bad.'

'Hence the scarf,' I said as I tied myself back together. 'It doesn't hurt.'

'I'll bet it did at the time.'

I laughed – a forced laugh, but I thought it would do. 'Why

do you find it so hard that I enjoy doing– Actually, no, that I enjoy *having it done?*'

She was quiet for what felt like a long time. 'Do you remember Cameron?'

There were very few things that Violet and I didn't talk about: Cameron was one of them. He was a teaching associate on my master's programme who knew no boundaries when it came to dating students. A straight white middle-class male, and the majority of the department were willing to turn a blind eye to his behaviour, for the sake of upholding their 'boys will be boys' ethos.

He pursued me and I did everything I could to actively encourage it. Violet and I had practically tailored an experience for the purpose of hooking someone back then – and it worked every time. I wore shorter dresses to his classes, stayed later to clear the rooms, and I was *always* the first to introduce a Freudian reading of a text. But when the plan finally came together – 'Agnes, why don't we take this elsewhere? We'll have more time at mine...' – Cameron hadn't wanted sex at all. Instead, he'd wanted someone to hurt him. And I hadn't known–

'Love?' Violet set her hand on my knee and gave a soft shake. 'Come back to me. Think about what's around you. What can you hear?'

Violet's voice; thrum of music; other diners; someone ordering a drink; Cameron telling me how to– I shook it away. 'Yes,' I snapped, then, 'yes, I remember Cameron.'

'Another drink?' she asked, for a rapid and welcome topic change. I sucked in a big breath, exhaled hard and murmured in confirmation. 'I'll order.' She stood and leaned across to set a soft kiss on my forehead. 'Then you can tell me all about Eliah.'

I felt my cheeks flush warm. *It pays to have someone who knows...*

CHAPTER EIGHT

A marriage is a contract. Over the years it's amended. Clauses are added and removed; certain information redacted with the promise of it never being mentioned again.

My surprise visits to Fin's office were a clause. Like a landlord demanding unscheduled visits to a tenant, I liked to know what people were doing with my property when I didn't reside on its arm – or something to that effect. I typically found him with his head buried between the pages of a tome, and that's where I expected to find him always. The visits, random though they were, were always scheduled around his timetabled classes; a strategic decision, thanks to the department secretary having supplied a copy of his timetable when I gushed about planning a trip away for us. I promised wholeheartedly that it would be mine and her secret and, bright though he may be, Fin had never thought to question how I always timed trips to coincide with an office hour.

On account of these visits being 'random', though, Fin could never truly prepare for an inspection. So when I knocked on the office door and shuffled in without waiting for permission one lunch hour, he didn't have time to do away with Dr Loughty: petite; pretty;

and perched on the far corner of the desk like a literary cliché. Fin's eyes spread before he tried to save the expression with a smile, while Irene stayed fixed to her spot as though already a trophy for him.

'Sweetheart.' He stood and closed the distance. 'This is a nice surprise.' While he kissed me on one cheek then the other, I watched over his shoulder as she finally stood up straight from her lean and smoothed down her skirt. 'What are you doing on campus?'

'Nothing, honestly nothing. But I've come into the city for some air, a little walk about the place, and I was so close when I hopped off the train that I thought I might as well, you know, pop by.' I craned around him to get a look at her. 'Irene, was it?' I wouldn't give her the status of using her title.

She leaned forward and extended a hand. 'The other Dr Villin.'

I flashed a tight smile and matched her gesture. She had the look of nerves on her. 'I didn't realise you were based in the same department as Fin.'

'Oh, I'm not but–'

'It's the same school,' he interrupted her. 'You know what it's like around these parts these days, they lump together all sorts of subjects whether they belong together or not.' I murmured agreement. I did know that – but I also knew Fin hadn't even given the good doctor a chance to tell me *what* she taught. 'You say you're in the city for a wander? Plans to see anyone?'

'I shouldn't think so. I'll visit the new display at the library, I might get as far as the art gallery. I don't suppose you're free?' I knew the right answer to this question. He shook his head, though, and gave the wrong one.

'I'm teaching this afternoon, sweetheart, otherwise I would.'

'Speaking of which, I need to get ready for an afternoon

class. Dr Villin, it's been lovely seeing you again.' She awkwardly stepped around us. 'The other Dr Villin...' She giggled and I wondered how Fin would feel at his demotion to *other*. 'I'll see you at the meeting? Late one again, isn't it?'

'Hm, can't bloody help themselves, can they? I'll see you there, Irene.'

She went light-footed down the corridor like a cat – or a vixen. One who'd just helped my husband to break a clause.

The hotel was a different one every time. It was the only way that either of us felt safe meeting in the city. I stepped into the foyer and gave a fake name – 'Mrs Parcell, Nicole Parcell.' – and rushed to an elevator once I'd got a room key. It wasn't until I was smuggled inside the space that I ever felt like we'd gotten away with it. If I could make it through the reception area without bumping into someone, I always believed we'd be fine. Eliah always took care of these bookings, though, and he valued his prenup agreement too much not to be careful about where we spent afternoons.

The lift ejected me out onto the ninth floor. The corridor was horror-film quiet and as I walked the length of it – Room 910 at the bottom – I wondered whether anyone else was having a sordid afternoon behind locked doors.

The room itself was an elegant one: cream furnishings and brilliant white bedding; the curtains part-drawn, but wide enough to show the cityscape outside. The walls weren't decorated with traditional artworks but rather colour-blocks; different shades of beige and brown that had been painted directly onto the magnolia, with a gold frame fixed around the edge of each square. It was minimalist. Nicole or Xara would probably know the term for it. *Christ, they might even know the names of the paint swatches.*

I ran a finger along the dressing table until I arrived at the phone docking station; I thumbed to our playlist before fixing it in the cradle. He was always happy when the scene was set for him.

There were thirty minutes still to wait before his final meeting for the day would finish. So I stripped free of my clothes and folded them over a chair for safe-keeping. Then I showered, lathered and washed away whoever I was when I was outside of a room with him. Nina Simone drifted in from the bedroom and I hummed along while I washed perfume scent from my hair; I'd pile it into a messy bun while I dried off. He'd told me before he liked natural curls on me.

The towel was already warm from a heated radiator. I swaddled myself in it, as though a self-soothing infant, and added a matching dressing gown to the outfit before I towel-dried my hair. When it was nearly dry, I fashioned it into a cinnamon bun at the top of my head. The bruises should have healed by now but they'd been deeper than I thought. It had been nearly a week since my drinking with Violet. But anyone could be forgiven for thinking the purpling was only days old still. There was foundation in my handbag somewhere, I thought, so I moved back into the bedroom then, sat at the vanity mirror and fumbled around in the side pocket of my bag. That's when the lock for the door clicked, a slide and beep.

Eliah laughed. 'Showered and ready?'

I didn't answer, only uncapped my make-up and added a pea to my fingertip.

'What did I miss?'

He threw his belongings on the bed; a gym bag that I recognised too well. When he was standing behind me, he kneaded at my shoulders like knotted dough and I felt myself soften under him. *What must it be like to have a man who comes home to do this?* I thought before reminding myself firmly that no matter what I thought others had, Eliah gave me this affection through drip-feeding – once a week. He pressed both thumbs at once into the base of my neck and my head tipped back. I shut my eyes and gave into the sensations, but somehow waiting behind my lids I found Irene. *Are they doing this at the moment? Is Fin this tender with her?* A laugh escaped then, because of course he wasn't. Fin didn't associate tenderness with lovemaking and that was a quality he heartily admired in his women. If they didn't like breath play before him, then they would by–

Eliah pressed into a bruise and my eyes shot open. 'Where are you?'

'Here.' I knew well enough that 'with my husband' was a poor admission when you were actively looking for ways to spend time with a man who wasn't him. 'I was just enjoying the touch.' I lifted my head upright but he pushed at my throat until I turned to an angle.

'That looks like it got out of hand.'

'You know bruises happen.'

He crouched, craned round to kiss my cheek. 'Why do you let him go like that?'

'Why do you let me?'

'Firstly, you never do this.' He touched a different bruise, softer this time, then I watched his reflection walk away. He yanked at the gym bag on the bed and struggled to find the zip. 'Secondly, I like the face you make when you're in that moment, Agnes. I like...' He'd been rummaging but he paused to face my mirror image. 'I like whatever it brings out in you.'

It saddened me to think he might see in me what I saw in Fin.

'I only have a couple of hours,' he added, then dropped

whatever he'd been holding. 'We don't have to do this at all, though, if you're not in a place?'

I pulled my hair free and let the beginnings of waves fall around me. *What will we do instead?* I wondered as I shrugged the gown loose. *Sit and talk about our feelings?*

Eliah stayed hovering near the bag, waiting for instructions. The equipment lived in his locker at work; the one spot we both believed to be safe from our spouses. And sometimes, when I needed the amusement of it, I wondered what would happen if someone made a phone call; threw an accusation: 'He's keeping drugs in that locker, I hope you know.'

'I'm good if you are,' I answered. But I set my hand on top of his to stop his searching. 'I don't need that.' Fin and Irene flitted through my mind again, and I smiled. 'I'll be fine with my hand.'

CHAPTER NINE

Despite Fin's assumption that motherhood mightn't be for me, I knew that did nothing for his want of a baby. I don't know whether he needed to be a father, or whether he only wanted an heir to boast as part of his assets. But I knew there were times when we were out together and I'd lose him to a pregnant belly; he'd eye a bloated woman like a teenage boy seeing tits for the first time to the extent that I worried what people might think, if they were to spot my husband the voyeur in action. Had the roles been reversed and *I* were the one making eyes at a stranger's stretchmarks peaking out from beneath a top that fit them in the second trimester, I knew it would seem only natural though. That's the main reason I left the behaviour to go unchecked in Fin; I'm nothing if not a believer in equal opportunities.

Still, he was so desperate for offspring, I sometimes existed at a point where I would have even given him one that weren't his – all for the sake of satisfying that craving for procreation. The first time Eliah and I had sex it was hurried; a frantic and frankly dangerous fumble while Fin and Nicole were both looking the other way. He panicked and mentioned the morning-after pill two days later. I assumed he'd been on a high until then. But I soothed him enough – 'Don't be silly, Eli, I'm on the pill...' – for it never to be mentioned again. I reasoned that it tipped the odds in my favour to be sleeping with both of them.

But ten days after we'd last seen each other, I crept from bed for a midnight bathroom break and found my underwear soiled with red-anger. I slipped one leg free then the other and dropped the unmentionables straight into the bin. They were white; some things weren't worth trying to save. I went to my cupboard, then, and ferreted free a packet of long fit Bodyform and a fresh pair of underwear – it was an emergency toolkit that every bleeder should have.

There was nothing different about this bleed to any other. I put on fresh clothing, stuck the pad in place and wiped away the beginning of a clot that had leaked. Not exactly pain, though, there was something in the base of my stomach that I realised after a moment or two wasn't disappointment at the discovery – instead I think it was relief.

'Agnes, what's going– Oh.' Fin pushed the door back without knocking and found me poised on the toilet, a glorified diaper between my knees. *Now that's a face of disappointment.* I hurried to pull my underwear up, but he turned quickly, as though shielding the dregs of my modesty.

'I'm sorry, I should have knocked.'

'It's okay, I... I didn't feel well.'

'Do you need anything? Painkillers? A water bottle?'

There was a lot of rage stored within my husband. Yet somehow, faced with the sight of a monthly bleed, he became a puppy eager to be trained towards the right behaviours. This was a routine we'd practised throughout nearly every period, and I'd come to think of it as his monthly outpouring of affection.

'Could I have some paracetamol?'

'Absolutely.' He stayed facing the doorway throughout, and before taking a step out of the room he added, 'I'm going to make you a bottle anyway, because it can't hurt. Would you like tea, as I'm boiling the kettle?'

I smiled. 'Please. With a sweetener.'

'Shout if there's anything else.' He was two steps out when I called him back. 'Yes?'

'I'm sorry.'

A sigh tumbled out of him and he dropped his head. 'I know.'

It passed within days; they always did. Alongside my inability to be a mother, apparently even bleeding properly was a hassle most of the time, too – despite the reports I'd made several times to our doctor. It was another thing he'd reassured me about once – 'Different women have different cycles and all.' – but the bitter fruits of it had been hanging since mine and Fin's first conversation about children. And there was too much shame in the extra details of my menstruation for me to readily part with them; not to either doctor or spouse. Still, the bleed itself was a reprieve from the violence of Fin's ordinary monthly feelings, and instead he was violently affectionate through it all. But one morning after, when he offered a hot water bottle and I replied with a thanks but no, thanks, he pulled the pin from a small grenade that I imagined must have been bulging out of his back pocket for days.

'I think we should talk about a few things tonight.'

I looked over the top of the book I was reading. 'What things?'

'A few things, Agnes, like I said. I'll be home at around six.'

'Will you have eaten?'

He thought for a second. 'No, I don't think I will have. You'll fix something?'

'I always do.' I was pretending to read by then. 'Have a good day at the office.'

It was emotional warfare: Fin knew I would spend the day worrying about the possibilities. His poker face was so refined that it was impossible to guess whether the things he wanted to talk through might be good or bad. For all I knew, he was readying to come home and ask for a divorce; announce the passionate love affair he'd been nurturing with Dr-bloody-Loughty. He and Irene might have been planning to run off to Boston together on an all-expenses paid research trip because Fin had finally decided that a wife who did nothing wasn't enough, even though that's how he'd made me!

I forced out a long breath and checked the time: 1.36. I'd killed time doing nothing, as with every other day. But somehow that day was moving slower.

In my wanderings to and from the living room window, I'd noticed that Nicole's car had been out for most of the morning but she was home now, and I flirted with the idea of calling her to arrange for an emergency dinner delivery. With the worry of the evening ahead sitting like a rockery in my gut, though, I decided the last thing I needed was someone who might take up residency in my kitchen and ask things like, 'So, special occasion?'

Still, there was no harm in sharing *some* of my discomfort. Of course, when I said sharing, what I meant was: to give someone else something to worry about, too. Or at the very least, I could give her something to overthink.

Nicole answered on the second ring. 'Hi, stranger. Coffee?'

'Hi, Nicole. I'm actually calling for a bit of advice. We're still relatively new around these parts but, I'm looking for a little quiet night in with Fin tonight, and I was wondering whether there were any hidden-gem food spots you could recommend.'

There was a long pause. 'Well, nothing beats a home-cooked meal.'

I smiled. 'It will be, just by someone else.'

'Well.' Another long pause. 'Eliah and I don't order in much. We don't have to.' She paused to let the comment hang. But one housewife can't leave another hanging; they're the rules. 'But when we do I know he likes to order from Bella's. It's an Italian café around a quarter of an hour out. They're very good, if you like that sort of thing.'

Of course, I remembered, *your husband and I have eaten from there before.*

'That sounds *perfect*. Sometimes you just want something done right, don't you? And ordering in is better than anything I can whip up in this kitchen, that's for certain.' I waited for a murmur of agreement from her before I added, 'Anyway, you're a doll, thank you so much. Tell Eliah I said hello? We should all have drinks soon.' I wondered whether she'd text him, snub my name for having sidestepped her countryside catering – or whether she'd start by telling the other wives, before him...

In the hours after I browsed Bella's menu, slowly sipped at white wine, and wondered how soon Eliah would know that Fin and I were having a romantic night in, to dine out from Eliah's favourite food place, too. *Okay, not quite romantic but...* That's how it would make its way to Eliah. Nicole wouldn't have a clue what she was doing either, she'd only be moaning to her husband about having been slighted for catering. I could imagine the ill-feeling unfolding in them both and it carried me through the afternoon. By the time Fin arrived back, I'd sipped my way through a third of a bottle and covered the dining room table with more pasta than any single couple could possibly eat in one sitting – and I felt good again.

Once we'd sat down he took a thirsty inhale and smiled. 'Bella's?'

I looked across to the kitchen island. 'You big cheat, you saw the wrapping.'

'That, too, but I like to think I have a nose for good food. Great choice, sweetheart.' He tucked a napkin into the top of his shirt and collected his cutlery. It crossed my mind that there was a ceasefire I didn't know about. 'I'm sorry for dropping things on you like I did this morning.'

But no, the bullets are coming. 'Things?'

'You know,' he twisted spaghetti around his fork, 'mentioning talk of things. I should have thought about you worrying all day with that.' He paused and fed the food into his mouth, then spoke around the softness of it. 'I more just wanted to make sure we had a proper sit-down together and a real conversation about things.'

'You're using the word "things" a lot,' I commented.

He nodded to my plate. 'You're not eating.'

'I will.'

Fin dabbed at the corners of his mouth and then leaned forward to rest his elbows on the table. 'Okay, perhaps we'll talk now, then.' He cocked an eyebrow at me as though challenging me to something. But instead of answering I swapped my measured sips of wine to a large gulp; audible as the liquid hit my throat.

'I've been doing some research into sterilisation. My understanding is that as a married couple, we're in a better position to make the decision for it than you would be on your own, as a single woman I mean, which seems wildly unfair but that's... Well, another battle for another day. As a couple, though, I think we're within our rights to ask for more information about it, at the very least, and I wondered what your thoughts were on the matter.'

I shook my head quickly, as though flinging the information into place. 'You want a vasectomy?'

His eyes spread wide. 'Christ, no. No, with your medical history in this already, it makes so much sense that, if it's something we opt for, you're the one to... You know.' He made a scissoring motion. 'Every month we put ourselves through the torture of expecting a positive test and I just– Frankly, Agnes, wouldn't it be nice if the option were just taken away?'

In the history of the world no woman has said, 'Yes,' in answer to that question and sincerely meant it. The last thing any of us wanted was *fewer* options for our lives.

'Why don't we just stop trying?' I tried to keep my tone steady.

'That's an option, too. But at least, if we know there's absolutely no possibility, then we know we can stop *hoping* for it.'

'Of course.' I speared a prawn. 'Do you need an answer now?'

'No, no. It's nothing to rush. Take a few days and perhaps we can revisit it.'

I flashed a tight smile. *As long as a few days.* Then I threw the food in my mouth, to give me ample excuse not to answer. And I chewed over that idea of giving up hope altogether...

CHAPTER TEN

E liah told me he needed time with his wife. I was Cool Girl enough to know I wasn't meant to react poorly to the sentiment. Still, it cut a little deeper than I expected when, from the window of my own unlit lounge, I saw Eliah and Nicole wrapped around each other in Dermot and Xara's front room. The four of them were gathered in plain view and I wondered what I'd done to be so spitefully cast out of couples' night. I checked my watch, then, and laughed. 'Maybe it's on account of not being part of a couple.'

Fin was late home again, and even though I hadn't yet gotten around to checking Find my iPhone, I knew I would. It was like having your favourite bottle of wine in the fridge, or the temptation of seducing someone you shouldn't: sooner or later, you always crack.

Dermot and Xara thumped down on the sofa, leaving only the backs of their heads visible. Eliah and Nicole stood in front of them and, in a fit of laughter, arranged themselves into prime position for what turned out to be couples' charades. Eliah was wearing a good husband mask, complete with a blue farmer's check shirt that he'd told me once he hated. Nicole bought them for him regularly because she thought they were in keeping with their aesthetic. The fact that Eliah spent his entire working week in the city wasn't a thing to hold her back from countryside cliché.

'Fucking hell.' I took a large mouthful of wine. 'What a thing to be banished from.'

I wondered whether Nicole could have felt so snubbed from my takeaway night with Fin, if that were the cause for my outlawing. *Or perhaps they're just bored of me...*

I shook the thought away.

The rest of my house was in darkness. When Fin texted me to say he'd be late, I hadn't even gone to the trouble of making dinner. I'd only brought in a fresh bottle, crawled into the window seat and waited for signs of life outside of it. Jessa and Umi had had their Friday night fumble already – the bedroom curtains closed at the same time at the end of each week – and there was a warm glow coming from the window of the room I knew was their kitchen. They might have been excluded from the couples' club, too, although it seemed unlike Nicole to miss points for diversity and inclusion. It was more likely that Jessa and Umi actually wanted to spend time with each other in private, I guessed, then I huffed a sad laugh. 'What a novel concept.'

My house stayed in darkness as the events of our little network unfolded because it made it easier to believe I were somewhere else. *Tragic, Agnes, tragic*, though I couldn't tell whether the voiceover was mine or Fin's. I watched the couples narrate film titles to each other – 'Because perish the thought that any of them ever crack a damn book.' – and drank wine until the sting of it started to bite at my throat. Two thirds of the bottle was gone, and I took an educated guess that they were perhaps only halfway through the night. *I need to slow this*, I thought as I reached down to set the glass on the floor. From this side of the window, I could see into the higher end of the village; the older side, we'd always called it, with residents who had been there since long before these modern builds were sneaked onto the land. Our two-storey cottage might have been given a thatched roof and some strategic timber work, but we knew – as well as every couple down this way did – that we didn't belong. The cottages and houses, a mere five-minute walk up from us all, were the authentic ones; structures that were built to last, that housed couples who had retired here for the quiet. Then we came with our motors and laughter from the big smoke. Fin had been so excited to leave behind the central city landscape, the apartment of mine that he'd moved into only twelve months before finding this place. Now we were here, and the city still had her fingers around his ankles every day that he chose to be on campus – which was most days, most weeks. I caved, then, and realised I needed to know who exactly was keeping him.

Fin thought he was the only one with Find my iPhone privileges, but it's easy enough to reverse search for a device. I waited for the map to unfold, the search to complete and–

'There you are.' I had no idea the faculty ran late night meetings at inner-city hotels. 'Christ, Fin,' I clicked out and opened Instagram, 'why do you have to be such a fucking cliché all the time?' I swapped out of my everyday profile – the open, no-secrets-here profile – and thumbed into the carefully tailored one. The one that didn't have a picture of me as the profile, but a picture of a plain-Jane mumsy type who would only ever want to follow other mumsy types – or mumsy bloggers sharing their tips for eventual dysfunction. It was an account that went unnoticed, though, and that's all I'd needed for it to be.

It was some time ago when the early suspicions of other women had started to simmer. But there had been something about Irene specifically at the department benefit. I'd made a note of her social media handles, then, knowing a night like this

might come. This great technology age of ours made it too easy
to know where people were – and with whom. Her profile
boasted pictures of academic textbooks, screenshots of
acceptances and pictures of a cat named Buttons.

The first time I'd accessed the display I hadn't treated
myself to a trip down memory lane, but that night I did; I had
nothing but time. It looked as though Irene were a fairly recent
graduate, with a doctorate graduation day timestamped as being
just four years ago. There was a picture of her alongside a young
man, too, holding each other in the way people do in the first
throes of romance. The caption gave further evidence for it; a
string of coloured hearts to spell out the location of the shot:
France, although there was nothing more specific. He didn't
appear any later than that one image, though, and I wondered
what had cracked them down the centre: someone else? Or was
it that Irene was such a career woman that once she got her
doctorate degree she upped sticks to a big city to use it?

By the time I was in the previous year of outdated images –
where I'd found another three featuring the same man – I'd
created a narrative that I had no evidence for. And I realised
then my composure must have slipped. I swallowed back
another rise of acid and scrolled up. There, the circle of her
profile picture implied there were recent stories to watch. I took
a long pull of air and reasoned that I could always block her
after viewing. So I clicked in and watched as a mound of
paperwork unfolded, captioned: 'The academic life.' The next
was a picture of an unopened bottle of wine with a timer:
'Nearly Friday.' I admired the restraint she showed, and it
crossed my mind that might be what Fin was attracted to. The
next picture was a closed office door – 'Out of office on!' – and
then the fourth, final shot: A bar. Two drinks on the table and a
jacket draped over the back of the seat opposite her own. I held
my thumb in place to keep the image on the screen, though it

didn't take me long to recognise the blazer I'd bought two Christmases ago.

'Should I be touched that you're even wearing it?' I asked, the question directed into the dull screen, while I tried to decipher what drink was in front of the table setting. There was hardly anything left in the glass, but I would have placed money on red wine.

BEFORE

While he was out of the room, I pulled three scented candles from my bag. I put one on his side of the bed, one on my own and the other by the closed window; they were all lit by the time he walked back in. He was holding a glass in each hand, and he stood dumbstruck in the doorway when he spotted the licks of light about the space.

'They're only candles,' I said, and tried to sound jovial with it. But he narrowed his eyes as though inspecting each taper for something more sinister. 'I'm not trying to integrate a feminine touch about the place if that's what your concern is.'

He'd told me in no uncertain terms – as many as four times, now, although it could have been more – that we weren't in a relationship, nor would we grow to have one. The first time he told me he broke the news gently, as though cracking an egg directly into cake batter and mithering at the prospect of shell flecks. Each time after, I'd thought he looked more disappointed than he perhaps should have done not to get a rise. It wouldn't have surprised me if he kept telling me, in the hope that my reaction might become something he could mop up with tissues and platitudes. The paperback leading male persona was never too far away, despite his kinks. *Could you have a kink for being the good guy in every situation?* I wondered as I leaned across and took the glass he offered.

'So what are you trying to do?' He landed in bed next to me.

'Cover up the smell of singed hair, mostly.'

He spluttered a laugh. 'Apologies, I know it's an acquired taste. Of sorts.'

'It's not exactly my first time smelling singed hair. I've had enough close calls with curling irons to know the scent of it. I've just never experienced it in the bedroom before.' When he didn't answer, I added, 'Does it sting?'

'It will for a while.'

'And it doesn't bother you?'

There was still so much I was learning; the level of discomfort that he could comfortably sit with was my main stumbling point, though, and I was desperate to jump the hurdle clear.

'Do you want to try it yourself, Agnes? It might help you.'

'Being on the receiving end?' I craned my head around to get a look at his expression. This was his first time offering a switch and I didn't know how sincere he was being. But it was also the first time I'd had such a fiercely negative reaction to something he'd suggested. I didn't leave pause enough for him to answer. 'No, I don't want to be on the receiving end. I like being where I am.'

He smiled and I wondered whether he'd expected that answer. 'Okay. Then let's stick with things as they are.' He paused to sip his drink, then extended an arm until I leaned in for a hug. 'Agnes, how long can you hold your breath...'

CHAPTER ELEVEN

Being other-ed had adverse effects on people. I think that's why I took the chance of seeing Eliah in his own home. The thought of soiling his marital bed was a bit too tempting – especially after the bliss I'd seen at Dermot and Xara's three nights before. He'd texted me to tell me Nicole was out for the whole afternoon: 'I know it's a risk. But...' She was at a charity event in Leeds. There was always a charity event somewhere. Meanwhile, my own spouse had spent the morning in his office and lunchtime with me, his head buried between the folds of a newspaper. It crossed my mind that in leaving the house I'd be giving him the peace that he so desperately wanted for the day. But he eventually made the decision for me.

'I think I'll go for a run.'

My head snapped up. I looked at him from across the table but he was still engrossed in his reading. 'You never run,' I answered. Then realised the error of my ways. 'Feel like something new?' I tried to lighten my tone and went back to shifting vegetables from one side of my plate to the other, as though I didn't care for his answer.

'We're getting to an age now, Agnes.'

We? I noted. *Am I meant to be swapping soft clothes for clinging ones and sweating my make-up off?*

'I just want to make sure I'm looking after myself.' I heard him rustle the paper, fold it down the crease and set it down. I looked up, then, and smiled at him. 'I've got a beautiful wife to keep myself in top condition for, haven't I?' He winked and stood without an answer. But he circled the table to kiss me, square on the mouth. When he pulled away I noticed the stain of my lipstick next to his smile.

'I might pop over to Xara's for a coffee. In case I'm not here when you get back.'

'Mother's meeting,' he said as he moved away, then froze, as though realising his error. He was facing away from me when he added, 'I... I won't be too long. An hour or so. Then we'll have some time together.'

I murmured in agreement and went back to my dinner plate. When the front door banged closed ten minutes later, I rushed upstairs to change into what I knew Eliah liked and left the house without warning him. There wasn't time for sweet love notes in whatever he and I had; we were geared towards efficiency, always. So I back-pocketed my phone in case of a Fin-emergency, crossed the street and knocked. He answered as though he'd been waiting, and we kissed like hungry teenagers right there in the doorway – as though neither of us had spouses in the wild. But soon I pushed him back into the house, slammed the door and let him take the reins on where we went next. We'd never been in his home before.

'Bed?' he asked, the word pressed against my warm cheek, and I smiled.

'Marital bed?'

'Don't ruin it.' He was pulling at my clothes. 'Get upstairs.'

The rush of it all made him more dominant than usual. He chased me up the stairs and steered me towards an open doorway. When I was faced off against the space though – the floral print sheets that were *so* Nicole; the wedding photograph on the nightstand, that I guessed must be her side of the bed – the reality of the homewrecking created a small storm in my stomach. *This is someone else's husband*, I thought, like it was only just occurring to me. *And you're someone else's wife.*

'Hey.' He stood behind me, reached around the zip of my jeans. I could feel the heat of his torso through my own clothes; he'd taken his shirt off without me even realising. 'You with me?'

I laughed. 'I think I've only just realised that you belong to someone else.'

He spun me around and stared through narrowed eyes, as though looking for something. 'Since when have I been anyone's?'

I rested the palm of my right hand against his Adam's apple and pressed softly. Eliah's larynx protruded more than Fin's did; not that Fin had ever let me touch him in the way I did Eliah. I felt the ripple of his insides when he swallowed hard.

'Not even mine?' I whispered the question close to his ear and felt another gulp. 'Get on the bed.'

And he did. It was that easy. There were two neckties next to the pillow and I smiled; *he'd got this all planned out.* Eliah didn't take control in the way that I did, but he was a forward-thinker. The first time Fin had done this there'd been no planning; I could tell from the way he reacted to his own force. He'd seemed so surprised that there was something in him that wanted to hurt me. But when I first pressed down on Eliah, months ago now, I hadn't been surprised at all by how much I wanted to hurt him; only surprised by how willing he'd been to let me, in a way that Fin wouldn't allow for. It was a different kind of intimacy, knowing you could damage someone; asking them to trust you not to. Eliah and I never talked about trust, but it was there – implicit. I tied his wrists, one after the other, to the bed posts. Then I kissed from his right hand down his forearm, along his bicep and settled next to his ear. 'Remember to knock three times.'

I waited for him to nod before I moved away to undress. He always watched; it was part of the game. There was no slow dance to it, nothing to make me anything more or different to what I was. With Eliah, I was only ever a woman rushing to have sex with a husband who wasn't hers. Normally I could set the thought to the back of my mind. But in the new space – the smell of Nicole's perfume, the nightdress discarded in the corner, as though flung away in a hurry – it was impossible to chase away the realness of it all. Even on Eliah, I was thinking of Fin. *Is he running right now, or is he with her?* I wondered, with my fingertips indenting around the soft skin of Eliah's neck.

'Never bruise me like that,' he'd said once, seeing what Fin had done to me nights earlier. I promised not to, for security's sake as much as anything else. But it had always been tempting. I wondered whether Fin thought of it as branding – whether that was my reasoning for wanting it, too, like a dog lifting its leg to piss on a lamp post: I have been here. This one is mine.

He fidgeted underneath me and I wondered whether his hearing had popped yet. It was always the first thing to go when Fin bore down. There was a build in pressure in me as though he'd created a physical stopper in my throat. Eliah and I had never compared notes but when I felt his innards gulp and duck and pulse as he tried to swallow, I wondered how much of our experiences were the same. His fingers twitched towards the wall and even though they didn't make it for a knock I still eased off. But he shook his head, rolled his eyes in asking, and I leaned forward again.

Fin told me once that a woman had done it to him. She hadn't asked beforehand, though, and there'd been no safe gesture, no glass of water by the bed. He always thought himself gentlemanly when he handed me a drink afterwards; I'd come to think of it as our equivalent of the after-sex cuddle – something we never did anymore. I glanced across to Nicole's bedside table again, then, and in place of a glass of water I saw the same wedding day shot as before. They were both young and recognisable, still. Nicole's grin was wide while Eliah's looked smug, satisfied with himself; a caveman taking home the beautiful woman. They looked so happy.

Knock. Ease.

'I'm sorry.' I looked back at him, then, but he only shook his head and smiled, then bucked beneath me in what felt like a playful gesture but I couldn't muster a laugh. Sex with Eliah had so often been escapism but there was something hard-edged now.

I tipped my head back to avoid his stare. Instead, I kept one hand gripped around him and balanced myself with the other flat against his chest. *Is this how she does it?* I wondered but then, *Which one of them am I thinking of now?* Nicole and Irene Loughty chased each other around my head like rowdy children; this game of catch and release. *Is that love?* I wondered, *Is that marriage?* And I squeezed around him tighter until my nails caught at his skin; he didn't knock, though, and I thought he must have lost the worry of me leaving marks behind. I didn't think I'd bruise him; Fin only stained me purple when he lost himself and I wasn't lost yet. Besides which, I wasn't amateur enough to leave evidence.

But God, this bedroom isn't the space for us. Knock. Every time I opened my eyes I caught sight of something that was tethered to the woman who really belonged here. When I tipped my glance back to Eliah I spotted a make-up stain on the pillow next to his. *Was she too tired to use a face wipe or had they been in that much of a hurry?* Knock. I tried to remember when Fin and I had last had sex, whether it had been in our marital bed or rushed against the nearest wall he could press me into. There were times when he didn't go to the trouble of chasing me into the bedroom. Knock. *Is he like that with her?* But I lost the persons behind the pronouns. *Who is he now?*

Knock.

There was a clock on what I guessed was Eliah's bedside table. He was the timely one out of the two. *Of course, consider how ready those ties were.* And I felt a flicker of resentment at the expectation in him. He'd *assumed* I would come. Though he'd been right, so maybe it would be more accurate to say he'd *known.* We'd been together for nearly thirty minutes already and I wondered how long Fin might run for. *Will he knock at Xara's on the way home to see whether I'm there?* But his ownership didn't extend that far anymore. Fin seldom showed suspicion; he was so certain that he'd made a circle of scent around me. Knock. He'd made rules easy enough to follow about the city and the friends and work, or lack thereof. How could he be suspicious of a wife so firmly under the thumb? *Under the palm,* I corrected myself and found that I was leaning down harder. Knock. And I couldn't even look at him, only think of Fin – and his rules.

It was a wonder that his wedding gift hadn't been to present me with a manual: Tips for being the best wife. All lowercase lettering because when we married I lost my rightful title; Doctor was relegated to Mrs and I still felt the blister of that in my belly, in the pouch where a child might grow if only I were a better *wife.* The word burnt like regurgitated wine and I wondered whether his sting of disappointment in me – Knock. Knock. – had helped to form the rules: *At least if she can't do* this *then I can make her do* that.

Knock.

But there were times when I broke them all: ignored the hurried taps against the wall; forgot the tall glass of water; decided to try two hands.

CHAPTER TWELVE

Solomon Burke's 'Cry to Me' flooded every speaker in the downstairs of the house. But I was grateful for any sound. There was no sign of Fin; the back door was locked and I'd had to unlock the front to get in. My hands had been shaking so much that I'd dropped the key three times. And as soon as I'd shaken my way into the hallway I hollered at Alexa to fill the space with anything. I wanted to sit, but the fear of leaving something incriminating in the domesticity of the lounge kept me loitering a safe distance from the room. *What kind of traces have I brought back here?* Instead, I let my knees buckle beneath me as I collapsed back onto the stairs, cradled my head, held my breath. *What the fuck have I done?*

Eliah was dressed from the waist up when I'd climbed off him. It had taken a lot to manoeuvre him back into his discarded shirt before I left. I'd unbound his hands and left the ties next to the pillow where I'd found them. And I inched his body onto the bedroom floor, as though that might hide the reality of what had happened. *What* had *happened?* I tried to re-piece it all in enough detail like it might make a difference. I was on top of him and– Knock. The wedding photograph kept creeping into my sight line and he– Knock. He writhed and bucked. But had that been before or after it started? His hips had jutted and– Knock.

In the lull between one song ending and another beginning I realised the knocking was real-time. I stared at the front door like there might be police behind it. The knocking wasn't frantic; it wasn't I've-just-found-a-body knocking. Still, it took two deep and steadying breaths before I could pull myself into a standing position. I grabbed the rail with a tremoring hand, yanked myself to standing and crept to the door as though I'd been relegated to the role of Queen Teen in a low-budget slasher film. *Only I'm the slasher*, I thought and a small animal-like noise fell out of me. I took another breath and shouted Alexa to pause.

The knock-knocking happened once more, and then I yanked the door wide.

'Gosh, I thought I was going to have to break the door down.' Umi stood there with a wide smile in place. 'Having a party?' She craned to look over my shoulder.

I forced a laugh. 'Sort of. Fin's out so it's just me and Alexa.' With a clap of thunder it came to me, then: *Be normal. This woman just became your alibi.* 'You know when you just want a dance around the house by your lonesome?'

'Boy, do I,' she said and matched my laugh.

My stomach rolled over and I set a hand flat against it, like holding something in that was too ready to spill out.

'Whenever Jessa has a late night at school it's my go-to to have the music blasting. It's up there with a lie-in and cooking dinner naked as far as I'm concerned. Self-care and all that.'

'Well, lucky you knocked before I got to that part.'

She let out a hearty laugh. 'I don't know that luck's the right word.'

Umi was one of those women who enjoyed idle flirtation

with others. It wasn't a sex thing. She'd flirted with Fin before now and I'd relished the discomfort he'd shown in his uncertainty of whether to flirt back. But Umi and I had passed compliments and comments back and forth more than once. And there wasn't much I wouldn't have done to make a good impression that afternoon – including stripping off and putting a slice of cheese on toast under the grill if that's what it took.

'You old charmer.' I reached forward and tapped her forearm softly. 'Anyway, all that knocking you've done, must be for something important. Is everything okay?'

She butted the palm of her hand against her forehead. 'Yes, entirely. Are you and Fin free this evening?'

'I... I honestly have no idea. Probably?'

'Jess and I were thinking of an impromptu get-together. Fancy it?'

I smirked. 'Do you plan on asking for keys in a bowl?'

'Oh, Dr Villin, if only you would.' She set a hand on the outside of the doorway and leaned into me. Umi was grey-haired before her time but the Cool Boy curled quiff made her every bit the fashionable lesbian stereotype. 'Seriously, though, we thought it might be nice to throw some snacks together, crack a bottle of wine...' *Act normal in front of credible witnesses.* I nodded along with all her suggestions. 'Check with Fin?'

'Sure. When he's back I'll ask him and I'll drop you a line. Are you inviting...' I petered out and nodded to the houses across the way from us.

'I want to invite Xara. Jessa tells me if I invite Xara then I have to invite Nicole. So, yes.' She rolled her eyes. 'Playground politics, eh? When will they cease?' She started to back away down the path, then, and I wanted to drag her into the house; flesh out my alibi; give me a reason to act like a person who hasn't just–

'Let me know when you've spoken to Fin? You can just turn up if you're game for it. Seven, or thereabouts.'

'Perfect.' I smiled. 'See you later.'

When the door was firmly closed I pressed my back against it and let my legs give way again. I rested my head to my knees and tried to take more deep breaths but there was no meditating my way out of this. There was a stifled sob moving up from my belly, hugging my shoulders until I felt them begin to judder with ill-feeling and before I could swallow it back down I found I was sobbing. Deep and heartfelt bursts of sentimentality as though I'd put down a beloved pet. I let out a strangled instruction for Alexa to fill the space with sound again and allowed myself the run of one song – Nina Simone crooning to 'Don't Let Me Be Misunderstood' – to sob, cry, confess. Then I would shower, I decided. Then I would be fine.

Fin fell through the front door, huffing and puffing like a criminal on the run from the authorities. From the kitchen I heard him panting his way between rooms and I smiled. I was dicing peppers like someone who knew what they were doing when he landed in the doorway.

'Bloody look at me!'

I followed instruction and the knife slipped from my hand when I saw him. 'Christ, what happened to you?' I turned and pulled the first aid kit from the cupboard behind me. 'When you'd been so long I just assumed you'd met someone on the route.' It was a lie; a bold and bloodied one. It hadn't occurred to me that anything might have happened because, not for the first time that afternoon, I'd been too busy thinking of a man other than my husband. 'Here, sit down.' I pulled a chair from the table for him and for once he followed my order.

He landed heavy and held his arms out like a child proudly displaying their war wounds. 'I took a right bloody tumble.'

'I can see that.' I got to my knees in front of him. He was still panting so was, I guessed, unable to fill in the blanks of what had happened. But I cooed in all the right places and apologised for the discomfort of dabbing disinfectant into his open cuts that ran like fingernails had been dragged down his skin. 'You look like you've been in the wars with someone big and bad.' I pushed myself upright and crossed back to the cupboard to find the most recently opened tube of arnica.

'You could say that.' He laughed, then added, 'Mother Nature knows her stuff.'

'Women often do.' I squeezed his knee as I crouched back down. 'There's bruising coming up there already, which is good. Did you want to shower? It might be best if we do this after you've washed. I can get a cold pack from the freezer first, though, if you're comfortable enough where you are?' I knew all the right treatments for helping the human body with dispersing bruises as fast as it was able. A cold press would help to slow down the blood. 'You could do with raising your arms a little, really.'

He grimaced and I wondered whether the discomfort was physical or emotional. *Does he feel bad that I know these things?* The disinfectant I'd dabbed so gently with fresh gauze, he rubbed in the rest of the way with grubby fingers – a child spurning their mother's efforts. But I only smiled and started to pack the contents of the kit back into the green box.

'Whatever you decide.'

'I think I'll shower.' I moved to stand up, shift clear of his way, but he set a hand on the ball of my shoulder. When I looked back he flashed a tight smile and added, 'Thank you, Agnes. You're always taking care of me.'

'I'm your wife. It's my job.'

After, I quietly packed the box back into the cupboard, washed my hands and grabbed the knife from the chopping board. Fin groaned, tipped his head back and rubbed at his eyes, but I didn't offer further sympathy. I was too busy nursing a low boil of self-pity for my own reckless afternoon.

'Umi invited us over for snacks and wine but I'll text her to tell her we can't go.'

He stood, then, as though the announcement had prompted something. 'Thanks, sweetheart. I think a quiet night nursing these,' he twisted his arms one way then the other to show off nature's defence wounds, 'in front of an easy-viewing film is probably what the doctor ordered.' When he got to the kitchen island he pulled his phone from his pocket and threw it down on the counter. 'The worst bit?'

'You've broken the screen?' I asked without looking up. Instead I speared through the skin of a red pepper.

'Nothing quite so tragic. But I took your phone with me and I don't know your passcode.' He let the comment hang; it had often been used against me as damning evidence for something. 'So I couldn't even get into Spotify *and* it looks as though you're the healthy one.' He circled around to me – where I'd frozen mid-slice – and kissed the side of my forehead. 'Apple Health might send you a notification in a second asking whether you're okay. What have you...'

I've been for a run. I rolled the idea around. *I'd been for a run when Umi–*

Fin clicked his fingers in front of my face to snap me back into the room. 'Agnes, I said what have you done with my phone?'

'Shows how much attention I pay.' I went back to cutting peppers to give my hands something to focus on, apart from the onset of a tremble that I could feel inside. 'I didn't even realise I'd got yours here. It'll be upstairs on the dresser. I've put clothes into wash, by the way, but it hasn't started yet if you want to add yours when you get down.'

Another kiss, this one accompanied with a light tap on my rear. 'So wifely.'

He left, and the thud of his footfall on the stairs felt like another clap of thunder: *Be kind to your husband.*

Your husband, who's covered in bruises.

Your husband, who's been here all afternoon.

Your husband, who you left here – while you went for a run.

CHAPTER THIRTEEN

I n the days afterwards everything went too fast and too slow all at once. No, we didn't see anything unusual; no, we didn't notice anyone coming or going; no, not a bad word to say about the man. Fin did most of the talking which I wagered was of benefit to me, given that I didn't know what might come tumbling out. It wouldn't have been a confession. But a clumsy accusation, maybe.

Instead, I avoided eyes with the detectives and nodded my head in agreement with my husband. I turned down the offer of adding anything else but said, 'Of course, please come round whenever you need to,' when a follow-up interview was mentioned. They took the names, addresses, and professions of everyone within walking distance. And we all gave ourselves willingly for their notebook to collect us. Suburbia has nothing to hide.

Nicole – every bit the heartbroken widow – was caught wailing outside the front door of her home, only once, but a concerned sister had swept in and snatched her away from the clutches of the crime scene soon after. The wives – or my allies, as I was coming to think of them – told me she'd been distraught at the news and she was recovering across the way in Leeds: a safe distance away. And I wondered whether the police would find that suspicious.

Five days after Eliah died, Fin came thumping down the stairs while his tie was still loose around his neck and I imagined–

'What's your plan for the day, sweetheart?' He kissed the crown of my head and scooted around me to fill a porcelain travel mug with black-tar coffee.

He'd been questionably normal. But that was a thought I'd had of so many people by then that I'd begun to wonder whether I was the one acting out of the ordinary. Like a woman who's just lost her lover, perhaps, which would be my excuse if I eventually needed one.

'Xara, Jessa and Umi are coming for breakfast.'

He choked on a mouthful of coffee; snorted, as though the drink had gone down the wrong way. 'Why?' he asked, mopping at the corners of his lips.

'Because we've all had a shock and we need to pull together in times like these.' I kissed his cheek and went back to browsing bakeries on my iPad. 'Do you know the name of that cake shop in the centre, the one that delivers?'

'You're getting cakes in?'

I kept my tone flat. 'Well Nicole likely won't bring any.'

'Nicole's coming?' he snapped and dabbed his mouth again.

'I was being sarcastic.' There was a long pause, then, and although I didn't know for certain whether he was watching me, I sensed a stare. I shook my head and sighed, then looked up at him. His eyes were glass beads with colour and no substance. 'I'm sorry. I shouldn't have... I'm sorry, love. All of this is so strange and unexpected and– God, it's just so terrible, isn't it?' I knocked my voice up a notch and forced my breath to catch. 'I'm sorry, Fin.'

I leaned forward to invite affection and he took the gesture as intended. He wrapped his arms around me and locked his hands against my back so he could pull me in too close. I rested my head against him then, my cheek against his neckline, and I juddered softly as though tears were coming – but the make-up had taken too long that morning for me to afford the situation real ones.

He patted my back softly – 'There, there, sweetheart.' – and pushed me away, held me by the shoulders at an arm's length. His eyes were narrowed, inspecting me for something. 'Are you sure it's wise to be spending time with the other wives today? You don't even like them, do you?' He dropped his touch, and went back to readying himself for work.

I watched his hands fumble with his tie, imagined my own–

'Wouldn't it be worth spending time with some real friends? I'm sure Vi would be around, if you called.'

I turned away, scrolled through the iPad's listings again. *This is a test I will not fail.* 'I think I'd rather be here. I know we haven't always seen eye to eye but we're all in this together, aren't we? Vi is so outside of it all.'

He kissed my temple. 'I suppose you're right, sweetheart. Be careful with them, though, won't you?' He moved around the kitchen as he spoke; grabbed his laptop bag; headed for the door. 'One of them might be a murderer for all you know...'

Because we were cultured, we kissed each other on the cheeks to say hello. I let my lips sit against Umi's cheek for a second longer than the others; small gestures, to seed our new friendship. They had filed into my kitchen where fresh baked goods were waiting, recently delivered by The Spinning Wheel bakery, although the evidence of that was stashed in the recycling bin in the garden. To cement my wifely status, I'd put the muffins in the oven on a low heat to keep them warm – and to smell the house out. Yankee didn't make a 'Here's one I baked earlier...' candle but the oven trick had worked. Xara and Jessa both inhaled deeply when they entered the room and Umi laughed – 'I didn't have you down as the traditional housewife type.' – but she also readily accepted my offer of fresh tea and a blueberry muffin.

'It's terrible, isn't it?' Xara said around a mouthful of pastry. My eyes shot wide and she rushed to apologise. 'Not the food! The cakes are all beautiful, Agnes, gosh, I'm so sorry. I only meant the situation.'

I caught my chest and feigned a laugh. 'I'm not sure I could take a criticism like that at the moment.'

'They're beautiful, Agnes.' Jessa reached over to squeeze my hand.

'Thank you.' I looked around them all then. 'Thank you for coming over.'

'If we knew you were so talented in the kitchen we would have been over before.' Umi winked at me as she helped herself to a second blueberry muffin from the tray in the centre of the table. 'Are you and Fin managing okay?'

'With the news, you mean?' I asked and she nodded. 'I suppose we're managing as well as anyone else. Xara, I mean, goodness, you were right next door.'

She swallowed hard and I imagined the raspberry jam filling of a pastry dropping into the well of her belly. 'We might have been right next door, but we didn't hear a bloody thing. How terrifying is that?' There was a murmur of agreement and I pursed my lips to hide any signs of relief. 'Umi had to bang the door down to get our attention when she came over about the shindig.'

'In the middle of something, were you?' Jessa smirked from behind her mug.

Umi caught my eye. 'I had to do the same for Agnes, too. Maybe it's me.'

'Oh, come on,' I tried to sound light, 'I'd just been for a run, I deserved a dance around the house to some music as a cool down exercise.'

'You looked pretty flushed to me.' She winked, and Jessa slapped her arm.

'Exercise will do that to you. Not that you'd know, Mrs!'

They fell into an easy conversation, then, about their exercise regimes or lack thereof. They asked how often I ran – 'It depends on the state of my marriage,' I joked, and they laughed – and I asked what workouts they did, whether Dermot was an exercise type – 'Men don't need to be, do they?' Xara answered and we shared a groan – and then someone floated the idea of a group workout. 'Thanks, but I'd rather group drinking or group shopping as a bonding exercise,' Umi answered. She was in brilliant shape, though, so her Cool Girl façade about not needing to exercise only lit a flame of annoyance in me. She wasn't a diet culture dropout, but she had the smugness of someone pretending to be.

The chatter rolled on until a full hour had passed – and nothing more was said about my run, or how Umi had only just caught me, or even how Fin had been out of the house at the time. Even though I'd practised saying, *I'm not actually sure where he was that afternoon*, four times in the mirror before the wives had arrived. No one seemed to care about the blatant lie I'd told them all about my run, either; that, or they only believed it to be an easy truth.

Xara's phone vibrated across the table's surface then and I jumped.

'Guilt got your back up?' Umi asked.

'If only.' I winked and I noticed the colour of her cheeks change.

'Oh.' Xara peered forward to check the screen but didn't move to answer. 'It's Nicole.' She glanced back and looked around us as though we were a consulting coven. She raised an index finger over the green, then the red, then asked, 'Am I the *worst* person in the world if I don't answer?'

Better or worse than the woman who killed her husband?

I waited for someone else to answer.

'Look,' Jessa leapt in with a soft tone, 'if you don't feel ready to talk to her, just leave it. She'll assume you're busy and you can call her back when you feel ready.'

'Besides, you're here and we're having a nice time,' Umi added, and Jessa was quick to give her a gentle thump on the upper arm. 'What? The world hasn't stopped and Agnes has gone to a lot of trouble to make this feast for us.' She locked eyes with me, and something in her face said it all: *She knows.* 'I really did never have you down as a cook, Agnes. You're much more domesticated than I had you pegged for.'

I picked up my empty mug. 'You make it sound like a bad thing.'

'And aren't *you* domesticated?' Jessa added.

'Me? Veritable member of the bad wives' club if only you knew it.' She pulled Jessa closer to kiss her cheek.

'This one would have you believe she douses herself in sugar goods and flings herself into a pool of hungry women every night if you listened to her.'

'I can think of worse ways to spend an evening,' I answered and there was a rumble of laughter again, although Xara's seemed less authentic that time. 'Does anyone want more tea?'

'I'll help.' Umi stood. I managed half a protest before she shut me down. 'Come on, lead the way and I'll help with teabags, sugar...' She waited until we were out of earshot from the other two before she said, 'I can help you break up the recycling box from The Spinning Wheel if you need help with that, too.'

I shot around with a lie ready on the tip of my tongue, but when her face broke out into a smile I lost it. 'You won't tell them?'

She leaned in and whispered, 'Our secret.'

I turned to fill the kettle and hide my own grin. I felt as though I'd been initiated.

CHAPTER FOURTEEN

There were no secrets among us anymore – apart from the cakes, that is. The detectives had no sooner left Xara's house and she was on the phone to me: 'The woman is nicer than the man, but isn't that always the way?'

I watched them leave, of course, and saw them tread the path of Nicole's front garden, push the door open like they were the new owners. *I wonder whether she'll move.*

'They said they had some business to take care of at the crime scene.'

I thought I detected a smugness in Xara, as though she thought herself part of the investigative loop all for happening to live in the first house in the cluster. 'They're going to make their way around the houses for much of today, I think. I already texted Jessa, but I know she's got Umi and I didn't want...' She made a huffing noise. 'I didn't want you being alone. Silly of me, really.'

Not silly, I thought, *though perhaps snide.*

'Xara, you're an absolute sweetheart.'

She laughed. I imagined her cheeks blushing rose. 'Not really. I saw the car wasn't there, though, and my Dermot isn't here either, so I thought we could keep each other company. I would have come over, but...'

'No.' I stepped back from the window when I saw the two detectives leave Nicole's house. 'You don't want them to think we're in cahoots.'

'We're hardly prime suspects though, either.' She guffawed. 'I wonder who is.'

'Have you heard from Nicole?'

'You don't mean to suggest she–'

'Goodness no, no, not at all,' I hurried out in a way even I partially believed. But seeding the idea wouldn't do any harm either, I reasoned. 'I only meant, it's been a few days since she called you, here. I've wanted to get in touch but... I don't know, I don't know how keen she'll be to speak to people.'

'I called her back, the evening we all saw each other, but truthfully it wasn't even Nic who answered, then; it was her sister. She said Nicole was sleeping. Something about sedatives? I can't rightly remember now. She was knocked out, though, so I sent my best and left a message for her to call me.' There was a long pause then, and when I glanced in the direction of the front of Xara's house I spotted her trying to get a view of two doors down. 'Can you...' she started and I filled in the blank.

'They went into Jessa and Umi's about two minutes ago.'

'Do you think– Oh bugger, Agnes, Derm is calling me. Let me call you back?'

I made non-committal noises. It was a good time to cut the call short, anyway. Since Fin had left two hours earlier, I'd only played at getting ready: half-heartedly blended foundation from face to neck; picked out a dress, and a decorative scarf; then I'd killed time at the window. But I didn't want the police to find me, sticky-palmed against the pane waiting for them like an orphan cast out of a Victorian novel; hanging on for the reward or the cane. I sighed. *I would always choose the latter.*

DS Elza Fendley and DC Wyatt Craw sat on the guest sofa, and I struggled to remember a time when someone else had done that. They were friendly enough – as detectives investigating a murder are, or can be, I supposed – and they assured me it was an informal chat, to try to get a better feel for the occupants of our huddle. They opened with questions about Eliah and I answered with audible thuds in my swallows, struggles in my breath and fillers of hesitation in my speech.

'I'm sorry.' I leaned forward to pluck a tissue from the box on the table. I wouldn't normally go in for that sort of clutter, but I'd thought ahead to the staging of this. 'I shouldn't cry, really.'

'It must be a very troubling time for you,' Craw commented.

'Your neighbours paint quite a pleasant picture of the place.' Fendley was looking out of the window as she spoke. 'It must be especially troubling, such a tight-knit community, having something like this happen right outside your front door.'

I pocketed my tissue, touched my neck and winced. 'You expect this in the city.'

'Your relationship with–' Craw started but Fendley cut across him.

'You've bruised your neck?'

I touched the area again. Before they'd arrived I'd put pale foundation on, to cover the severity of the purple that was blooming below surface. But then I'd brushed a light red in its place to strike up the appearance of bothered skin. It was the same red I used on my cheeks for cocktail parties and departmental elbow-rubbing: the glow of someone two drinks in from the moment I arrived. With the right brush, though, it became the same colouring as skin that's felt a recent pressure.

'Only bruising.' I pulled the scarf awkwardly around me as

though to cover the shading. 'I fell at an awkward angle while I was out running, the day Eliah... The day in question.'

'That was some time ago now, Dr Villin, I'm surprised the bruising hasn't faded.'

I huffed a laugh. 'I'm not that sort of doctor, I'm afraid. I can't comment.'

'Where did you run?' Craw asked, a pen at the ready, and Fendley shot him a look of annoyance. They were an unlikely and improper pairing; everything I'd hoped the police might be.

'I can show you, actually.' I lifted myself up and pulled my phone from my pocket. 'I use one of those godforsaken Find my Phone whats-its, but it tracks your fitness progress, too. Although, since that run a few weeks ago I haven't felt altogether comfortable being out in the sticks for long periods.' I handed the phone over to them. 'That midway point is where I tumbled. It wasn't bad, but I took a break there for a while, caught the scenery, then I took a slow run home.'

I sat back in my seat: *Nothing to hide here.* Fin had told me the route he'd run along on the day of Eliah – 'Bloody council should be ashamed of that hillside.' – and he'd underscored, several times over, how the fall had been due to overgrown greenery blocking a path. Two days later, I'd taken a slow walk along the same trajectory. I wasn't much of a runner. But if they asked–

'Is this your usual route?'

I snapped back into the room and smiled at Craw. 'Truthfully, I only run occasionally at the best of times. I've run that route once or twice before but the greenery up there was a little tamer when I last went, hence...' I gestured to my throat. 'I landed at such an awkward angle, you'd wonder how I managed it.'

Craw was busy noting something down, still, but Fendley was looking right at me. The stare from her was something unsettling, and I wondered whether this was a technique she used often, or whether the intensity was something I'd brought out of her.

'Can anyone provide an alibi for the time you were running?' Craw asked, then.

I'd known this was coming. But still my stomach turned over like an angry wave storming the beach. 'I mean, my phone does, surely? But one of my neighbours, too, I suppose. Umi, you might have met her?' I gestured beyond the window but when neither of them answered I added, 'She caught me having a bit of a wind down. Sweaty-faced and dancing around to whatever Alexa happened to be playing at the time.'

Fendley's smile was tight. 'She mentioned.'

So you're checking us all over then...

'Your husband.' Craw pushed my phone across the table, back toward me. 'Where was he at the time?'

I looked between them both, and I tried to fashion my face into something that I hoped would look troubled. 'I can't say. I mean, I'm not sure I quite know.'

'He was out?'

'I...' I let the sentence die on my lips. 'Yes, but I can't say where. You'd have to ask him, I'm afraid. Let me think.' *One. Two.* 'He certainly wasn't here when Umi came over, about the drinks in the evening. He may have already been out when I left for my run, too. He spends a lot of time in the city these days, on the university campus.'

'On a weekend?' Fendley asked and I arched an eyebrow.

'You'd be surprised.'

Craw noted something down. 'We'll be talking to everyone from the neighbourhood in due course so that's no problem, anyway.'

I skirted around mine and Eliah's relationship with strategic non-answers, followed by a run at overstating my feelings towards Nicole and the rest of the coven. I was a mere inner-city housewife who had been taken in by a local flock and goodness, wasn't I grateful for it?

'You're close?' Craw asked.

'Strangely, this has brought us closer I'd say.' It was at least an answer that I wagered the others might agree with – assuming they hadn't felt moved, even, to say it themselves. 'I can't speak for Fin's relationship to this place, but I feel as though I've settled so much more recently, anyway, and now myself and the others... They're a great support, that's all I can say.'

'Your husband doesn't like the country life?' he asked, and I thought it was more a question from curiosity, rather than anything that stemmed from the investigation.

'He spends a lot of time out.' I flashed a tight smile and added, 'Back in the city.'

Fendley soon initiated the end of the interview, though, before Craw had the chance to ask anything more of our personal lives. She thanked me for my time and, when I asked when they might be visiting my husband, she only said, 'Soon.' It made me warm to her, that tactical secrecy she could pass off as work while I could only pass it off as preservation. *What's the rush?* I thought, as I walked them to the front door. *He isn't a suspect, yet.*

Craw was a couple of steps down our preened path but Fendley lingered in the doorway. 'We'll be in touch if there's anything else we need. But feel free to call me if anything comes back to you?' She handed me a neat business card. 'You'd be surprised the details that rush back when you take a second to think.'

I accepted the offering, but before I could add a platitude she pointed to my neck, and added, 'You should think about getting that checked, Agnes.'

CHAPTER FIFTEEN

One of the few instances where I wouldn't demand that people use my proper title was during healthcare appointments; when I was in the presence of *actual* doctors who help people. Meanwhile, the likes of Fin and myself were only ever likely to diagnose fundamental problems with the patriarchal dominance of British writing between set periods, and/or problems with the earth's core. I couldn't decide which one of us proved more useless in a medical emergency. Although, the doctor I managed to book an appointment with that afternoon could have rivalled mine and Fin's uselessness any day of the week, if the speed at which he read my medical notes was an indicator of the proceedings. He had one of those hard-to-read appearances that placed him anywhere between twelve years old – unlikely, though students were getting younger each semester – and thirty-two.

'You've had some fertility issues, I see.'

The comment stunned me. I said only, 'Yes.'

'You're under a Mr...'

'I'm not here regarding fertility issues.'

'No,' he answered, in a tone that suggested he didn't *actually* believe me.

'I'm having some discomfort with my throat.'

'Ah.' He pushed back from his desk and rolled his chair to stop in front of me. 'Let's have a look, shall we?'

'It's not so much soreness in the actual throat that's the pro–'

'Well, let's have a look all the same.'

I opened my mouth wide. He grabbed a depressor and forced my tongue with an urgency that made me want to gag. Seconds later, he grabbed a small flashlight, shone it about in my gaping trap and said, 'Say ah for me, if you don't mind, Mrs Villin. A good long–'

'Aaaaaaahhhh.'

'No signs of an infection.' He switched off the small light and dropped the depressor in a nearby bin. Then, in a gesture that I'm sure no one has performed since the days of *Carry On Doctor*, he cupped his hands together and blew on them. 'Apologies, it's freezing in this office. I'm sure you don't want cold hands on you.' I murmured in agreement as he placed his fingertips gently on my neck. He pressed softly from just behind my ears, down my jawline, first, then along–

'Sorry, was that uncomfortable?'

I flinched when he reached where the last of the bruising was. The area wasn't peach skin tender; the colour of the misadventure had long gone, too, unless you were in the right lighting. But when he'd pressed in, then, I certainly felt the pinch. 'It was sensitive there, when you pressed.' He pressed again, as though to be sure, and I grimaced. 'Yes, still uncomfortable.'

'Hm. It looks here like there's signs of...' He moved from one side to the other, then back again, then back– His eyes shot wide, and I wondered whether, like a forensics expert sweeping a scene, he'd found signs of fingerprints. 'Mrs Villin, have you injured yourself at all in the recent weeks? Any trauma to the area?'

I gave him a searching look and narrowed my eyes. They give you agency when it suits. 'I'm not sure what you mean by trauma. I...' I reached up to touch where he'd touched, but pressed with a lighter hand. 'My husband and I...'

His expression changed at the mention of a husband alongside a bruise. They probably had a special seminar on these things now: a crash course in caring for the vulnerable and deviant.

'I mean, I was out running a week or so back and I took a fall. I could have... I suppose I could have fallen at an angle.'

He didn't look convinced. 'It seems unlikely that a fall would have...' He shook his head, though, and decided not to force the issue. Without any further prodding, he pushed over to his desk and went back to staring at the computer. I wondered whether he was looking for a history of domestic violence. I should have thought ahead. 'Have you suffered with this sort of discomfort before? Husky voice, tenderness rather than bruising, difficulty swallowing?'

I'd only reported one of those symptoms – tenderness, that is – when I called for the appointment. But I was grateful he'd gifted me the others. 'I'm occasionally husky in the morning, but my husband tells me that's normal. Swallowing is only difficult when the tenderness is there.'

He nodded slowly. 'I think I see.' I wondered whether there was more coming, so I stayed quiet and focused only on the wallchart opposite. I thought concentrating on the letters might give me a vacant stare. 'Mrs Villin, I'd like to keep an eye on this. Would you mind coming back to see me in a week or so?'

I shook my head lightly as though snapping back into the room. 'Why, sorry?'

'Only so we can keep an eye on that bruising there.' He gestured towards my throat. 'There's something amiss that I think is worth checking. Would it be okay to book you in for a follow-up appointment? The same sort of time next week, if you're available for it?' He started to click about before I answered, and I let myself be carried along. 'I'm going to prescribe a very mild antiseptic wash I'd like you to gargle with, in case there's something lurking that I haven't spotted. I'll send that straight through to the pharmacy.' Again, he didn't look up for me to answer so I didn't interrupt. But he glanced my way seconds later when he handed me an appointment card that he'd hastily scribbled a time and date on for the following week. I'd already decided I would call to cancel – in a husky voice.

'Thank you, Dr Moore.' I stood and smiled at the ground, every bit the downtrodden woman. 'I really appreciate your time.'

There was a suitcase in the hallway when I got home. I downed my knee-jerk reaction quick enough to realise it was one of his, not mine. The small one, which could either mean hand luggage for a flight or a short overnight stay somewhere – two nights, maximum – that he hadn't yet told me about. I wagered on the latter of the two options, and conjured another guess: *He's going to tell me I knew about this already.* There was the knock and clatter of coffee being brewed in the kitchen, accompanied by the hum of low music. I shut the front door with some force, to announce my arrival, and trod the length of the corridor to find him. That darling husband of mine was dancing around the kitchen island, coffee pot in one hand and empty mug in the other. The Big Dick Energy of him spoke volumes: he was either a man who'd just had sex, or one who was about to.

He laughed when he saw me. 'Sorry, sweetheart, running on caffeine.' He lifted the pot to underscore the comment. 'Drink?'

I made an effort to make my voice husky. 'Tea, please.'

'You're unwell?' He set the mug down and reached across to Alexa to lower the volume. 'What's wrong?'

'It's only a sore throat.' I closed the distance between us and eased the coffee pot out of his hand. When it was squat on the island behind him, I pressed him back against the counter, too. 'It's nothing that some quality time with my husband won't cure.' I rested my hips against his and leaned until I wagered the edge of the counter must be cutting in hard against him through his T-shirt. When my back curved, I felt the shift in him, too, and I wondered what his reaction would be: would he still go to—

'Sweetheart.' He put a hand either side of my waist and I couldn't decide whether he hoped to move me or measure me. 'I have to be out of the house in...' He craned around to look at the wall clock. 'Ten minutes.'

I kissed the space just below his ear. 'We've done it in less.'

A hard huff fell out of him, one I recognised as enjoyment. He moved his hands, then, to seek out my own. But there wasn't any handholding. Instead, he wrapped his fingers around my wrists and pinned them to my sides.

'You're a temptress.'

'That's why you married me.'

He laughed. 'Actually, I married you because you're a fine woman.'

What does that even mean, husband?

I smiled and leaned in to kiss his jawline. 'Be late.'

'Agnes...'

'Come on, where do you even have to be?'

Something in him tensed. 'I've got that work trip, I told you.'

There it is. 'I don't remember a work trip.'

He pushed me away, softly, and kissed my forehead. 'It's on the kitchen calendar, sweetheart, I did tell you.' In the small distance he'd created between us he managed to wiggle free and go back to his coffee-making. 'I didn't realise the time when I started this. Can you pass me a travel mug from the cupboard?'

I did as Fin instructed. But on my route around the kitchen, I made eyes at the shared wall calendar: 'F. Away. 2 nights.' It hadn't been there when I'd left the house earlier in the day, though; I would have bet his life on it.

He didn't speak again until his mug was full. 'I worry about your memory sometimes, Agnes.' I couldn't decide whether he sounded worried or jovial, though, so I waited quietly for whatever more there was. 'Should you see someone, do you think?'

'I think as long as I don't have to give anyone an alibi then we're probably safe.'

He huffed a laugh. 'Speaking of which, are you going to be okay here? Alone?'

Does it matter? 'While you're away, you mean? I'll be fine, Fin, but thank you.'

'You could invite the wives over.' He definitely sounded jovial that time.

'I'm sure I'll find company, Fin, don't worry.'

'Meaning?' he snapped. But I'd turned to reach for teabags and I pretended not to hear. 'Agnes,' he said, firmer.

'The wives, Fin, like you said.' I didn't turn, but made a slow effort at setting my tea to brew. 'You didn't say where you were going, did you? On this trip?'

'No, I didn't.' He came to a stop next to me, set the coffee pot down and rested a hand on my back. 'You're sure you'll be okay?'

'I'll call Xara as soon as you're out the door.' I looked up at him and smiled. 'I'm a real little housewife now, aren't I?'

But he snorted, cocked an eyebrow. He was right not to believe me.

CHAPTER SIXTEEN

Since Eliah, I'd stayed too busy to consider it all in any detail. But when Fin had gone there was no amount of music that could fill the quiet panic. I'd been so set on what I was doing, this was the first time I'd paused to consider what I'd done. I thought of him then though, of what it had been like to– Knock. His face had changed so quickly when he'd realised. His body had bucked in a way I'd recognised, too, from better times spent together and– Knock. He must have expected me to stop. I wondered whether he'd had time to realise– Knock. Knock. Could he have known I was about to–

Is dying worse if you know it's about to happen?

I uncorked a bottle of red and left it on the counter to breathe. I should have done it hours ago, but I'd lost so much time wandering around like a lost lamb or maiden. Thinking never did anyone any good. I was scoring through the crust of a loaf when the front doorbell rang and I jerked with such a force that I nipped my finger. The blood wasn't quick enough in running, though, and I caught it with my mouth when it had only just escaped the skin. I was sucking my finger when I opened the front door.

'I didn't realise it was that sort of evening.'

I spoke around the digit. 'I cut myself.'

'Let me?' She eased my hand away from my mouth and towards hers. She didn't lick it, though, only kissed alongside where I'd been nursing. 'All better.'

'You're a terrible flirt, Violet.'

'And you're a wicked tease. May I?' She glanced down at the step into the house. 'I think I need a formal invitation before I'm allowed to—'

'Shut up and come in, you strange creature.' I turned and walked back along the hallway. Vi must have stepped in behind me because I heard the door close. But there weren't any follow-up footsteps. When I turned, she was inspecting the corridor, looking through doorways as she took her time in getting to me. 'You're not Alice.'

'You mean to say the Red Queen won't try to behead me?' she answered, but her glance was leading up the staircase. 'Where is he?'

'I don't know.'

Her head snapped around. 'Floated his body down river?'

'Business trip. Two nights away.'

'Bollocks.'

'I know. You'll stay?'

She made a dramatic gasp. 'A whole evening with you?'

I turned and wandered the rest of the way to the kitchen, then, and she followed. 'Don't ruin it, Vi. Red or white?'

'Red. Have you eaten?'

When I turned back with two empty glasses at the ready, she was perched on a stool at the island, already familiar in the space. Vi had always had that confidence about her; she could exist in any room like she belonged there. It wasn't something that had come with age or intellect; from memory; this had always been who she was. She was thumbing through her phone, I guessed, to find a takeout place that would deliver. Meanwhile, I poured a generous measurement of wine into each glass globe. I took two hungry mouthfuls and spoke to her dipped head.

'What would you do if I told you I'd killed a man?'

'I'd say it's about time.' She didn't even look up. 'Are you okay with pizza?'

'Nothing meaty. Vegetarian supreme or something else colourful.'

'Done.' Seconds later she threw the handset onto the work surface and reached over to grab her drink. 'Are you thinking of killing Fin or is this a hypothetical drama?'

'I couldn't kill him.' *But I could frame him...* I took a gentler sip and winced when I swallowed. I needed to seed these things, I'd decided. I needed the idea to take root.

'Rough night? Speaking of, how does it feel living with a crime scene on your doorstep?' She cocked an eyebrow and took a sip. I tried to make it look like I was putting real thought into the answer. Rather, I was trying to keep my mouth shut from blurting out the truth of it all. Around Vi, I really didn't know what might fall out – or how she'd react to it. When I didn't answer, she added, 'I assume you've told the police you were sleeping with the victim.'

'Do you think I'd still be married if I had?'

Her eyes widened, only a flicker. 'You really haven't?'

'I'm terrified to, Vi.' I walked around and sat alongside her on another stool. 'Can you imagine what life will be like if I tell them?'

'Love...' She reached for my hand and tucked her fingers into the empty spaces of my own. 'Can you imagine what life will be like if you don't? You've a controlling husband who enjoys breath play and then mysteriously the man across the way, who you happen to be sleeping with, winds up dead by strangulation. Asphyxiation. I don't have the details. But you see my point, love, surely you do.' She paused to wet her lips with wine and in the kitchen lighting the red of it on her mouth looked like blood. 'Are you trying to tell me the thought hadn't crossed your mind until now, Agnes?'

I wanted to smile but I bit it back and pursed my lips instead. 'Isn't my home stunning?' I said with a break in my voice.

Vi flashed me a sad, sympathetic sort of smile that I imagined she typically reserved for patients. 'Fucking stunning, love. It's the best decorated penitentiary I think I've ever seen.' There was a smirk brewing and I wondered whether she'd keep a straight face long enough to finish accusing my husband of murder. 'I will always support you, Agnes, I always have. But you're a foolish girl if you don't protect yourself in this situation, and you're far from a foolish girl.'

I took two generous swigs then swallowed a third time to wash down the acidity in my throat. 'If you loved someone, would you provide them with an alibi?'

'In a murder trial? No.' She didn't miss a beat. Then added, 'But if it were you?'

It wasn't the first time Vi and I had talked in these hypotheticals – though it was the first time in a long while. I'd already known her answer, of course; there wasn't much she and I didn't love each other enough for.

'Let's change the subject?' I asked and she nodded, then raised her glass in further agreement. 'You look beautiful. Did you expect to go on somewhere else after you'd seen me?' Her hair was wound in a tight coil, perched at the crown of her head, and her make-up was pale, making the red of her lipstick and the wine even more pronounced. The rest of her was blackened. She wore a high neck jumper that showed her figure; not so tight that it looked deliberate; black, skin-tight jeans; knee-high black boots with a cream trim. 'I don't mean to keep you from a hot date.'

She snorted and reached across to tap my knee. 'You are my hot date. Is there a tour to this place?' She glanced up at the ceiling. 'Now I'm finally here.'

'Of course!' I grabbed the bottle of wine to top us up. 'Where would you like to start?'

'Upstairs...'

Vi and I didn't get further than loitering at the bedroom window. Across the road Eliah's house was in darkness; Nicole was still staying with relatives while she recovered. *Assuming she ever recovers from this...* The thought had reeled across my mind several times over since Vi cracked open the conversation of what it was like to live across from where he once lived, and I couldn't shake the wonder at what I might do with a death house that my husband had been killed in. That is, unless I chose to make a celebratory shrine of it. But I sensed Nicole and Eliah had had a better relationship than that. Vi played professional with every bit of information I gave her and tried to dissect the details that were available. But I knew she wouldn't guess the truth of it all. If I wanted her to know I'd have to tell her, and by the end of the second glass of wine – with still no pizza in sight – I felt dangerously close to upchucking a confession at her feet.

'Where are you?' she asked.

I nodded to the dark house. 'Over there, mostly.'

She reached up to push stray hairs behind my ear and the intimacy of it sent a shiver down my back. The last person to touch me with that sincerity had been Eliah. I felt the beginnings of a teary moment labour my breathing then, as I thought on the reality of missing him – which, not for the first time, I realised I did. And the duality of missing something that you yourself had snatched away or ruined felt uncomfortably human. *Do other murderers feel like this?* I shook my head at the M-word. I seldom used it.

'You must miss the connection you had with him.'

I nudged her. 'Don't analyse me, Vi.'

'I can sympathise without analysing.'

'No.' I turned to face the room instead and leaned back against the windowsill. 'No, I don't believe you can.'

She followed my motion, turned, then left a long gap before she said, 'It really is a beautiful house. You've done wonders with the space.'

'You've seen three rooms,' I answered flatly.

'I stand by what I said.' At the sound of a car she faced the window again. 'Headlights turning in, dinner must have arrived.'

She made to move, but I snatched her hand before she could get too far away. 'Vi, do you really think my husband has it in him to murder someone?'

She came back to kiss me gently on the side of my head. 'I think everyone does.'

BEFORE

I was on my second read-through of J. G. Ballard's *Crash*.
He'd lent me his copy to begin with but then I'd bought my
own. I wanted to dog-ear, highlight, scribble; steam the pages in
the bath and press them back together by wedging the book
beneath a textbook for a day. But on this second read-through,
I'd read the final twenty pages aloud in a room lit only by
candles, while he struggled to breathe comfortably after being
bound with his arms stretched at a crucifix angle for nearly
three hours. He told me the game was I could tie him, bind him
and do whatever I pleased – so I left.

His wrists were fixed to the corners of his bed while I went
into the city and caught up on essential shopping. To draw the
process out, I'd had a coffee and allowed myself the luxury of
reading for enjoyment; though I hadn't read *Crash* in public for
fear that someone might know it for its unsavoury nature. And
when I'd eventually come back to him, nearly two hours later,
the strip of tape across his mouth prevented any slurs from
coming – though from his eyes I could see that I wasn't his star
girl, then. But still, when I settled down with the book and two

fingers of white wine to sip through, he hadn't knocked – the alternative to our safe word – so I hadn't rushed.

When I sat astride him and peeled the tape away, he slapped his lips like a man starved of water for days. I reached over to the bedside table and picked up the wine I'd poured for him, and I fed a straw into his mouth for him to drink.

'Anything could have happened,' he said, with something bitter on his tongue.

'Hm.' I leaned forward to undo one of the ties. 'Exciting, isn't it?'

He laughed. 'You seem to be getting a taste for this.'

'I'm starting to learn the rules.'

'There aren't any rules, Agnes, *that's* what you need to learn.'

'I think given that I've taken myself on a quiet date today while you've been spread-eagled at home, alone, some might say that I'm already doing quite well for myself when it comes to this little arrangement.'

When both hands were free he pushed himself into a more comfortable sitting position, with me still atop him. He kneaded at the red circles that had formed like handcuffs, and I swallowed the urge to apologise.

'You're learning what you're capable of, that's what you're doing.' He reached around to get his drink, then, and drained the glass. 'I'll get us some more.'

'What do you mean, *what I'm capable of*?' He hadn't lifted me off him yet; I wanted to see his face while he answered. There were times when he said things from spite, or playfulness; then, there were times when he was frighteningly sincere. I never knew whether we would land on heads or tails, though.

He pushed my hair away from my face and cupped my cheek. 'All of this is just a start, isn't it?'

I nodded without knowing whether the question was rhetorical – or whether I agreed.

'I want to know what happens when you really let go, Agnes. What happens when you lose yourself?'

It was a valid question, but I was more concerned with two counter queries: *What happens if I get too lost?* Or worse still, *What happens if you don't like what we find?*

CHAPTER SEVENTEEN

I let Vi think it was her idea. For a woman with a notably complex understanding of the id and the ego, she'd never been especially equipped to know when her own were being pandered to. That, or she did know and simply didn't care. Still, on the second day of Fin's 'business trip', Vi near as damn walked me into the police station with her hand wrapped around my own. She stayed on the phone with me for the car journey from my front door to the car park, and when she heard the engine cut dead she offered, again, to be there when the confession was made. *Not* that *confession*, I had to keep reminding myself. But I declined her kind offer again and told her that if I needed her I'd call.

'Remember, love, you're doing the right thing in giving them this information. *All* of the information.' She leaned heavy to allude to the evidence I'd told her about two nights ago; more fine-tuning that Fin didn't know existed. But he would, soon. 'Call me when you're out, or when you're home. You're sure you don't want legal representation there? Because I can make a call to–'

'I'm fine, Violet, but I would like to get this over with.'

'Of course. Call me.'

She hung up, then, without waiting for my goodbye, and I dropped my head against the seat behind me. Only hours earlier I'd called the station to say I had information that I thought would be pertinent to the case and only minutes after that Fendley had called me back to ask how soon I could be there. But as I grabbed my laptop, exited the car, and closed the gap between me and the awaiting interview, I wondered again whether this was the right thing to be doing. I nearly laughed: *the right thing*.

The right thing would have been to have stopped when–Knock. I shook the noise away. The proverbial out-damned-spot had started to plague me like tinnitus for the last two days and I wondered whether it was an auditory hallucination; when guilt comes knocking, literally. Whether it was guilt over Eliah or guilt over Fin, it was too soon to say still. And I likely wouldn't know for certain until I'd handed over the information to Fendley and her underlings. *Catch 22*, I thought as I pulled the door and crossed the threshold into the station. I walked straight into DC Craw – *Has she had you waiting?* – which made backing out that bit more impossible, and I found that I was glad of it.

'Dr Villin, nice to see you again.' He held out a hand and I matched it. 'This way? There's a lot of traffic in the interview rooms today so we'll be a little further down the way...' There were peaks and dips in his volume as he hurried away from me and I struggled to follow, until he eventually came to an abrupt stop. 'DS Fendley is through here.' He pushed a door open but stepped aside for me to lead the way. 'I'm just about to get myself a coffee. Can I get you anything before we settle down?'

I locked eyes with Fendley as I answered her junior. 'Water, please?'

'No problem.'

'Thanks, Craw. We won't start without you.' She flashed him a thin smile and then the door dropped closed behind me. 'Come in, Agnes, please. Make yourself comfortable.' She huffed. 'It seems a silly thing to say but...'

'I appreciate the sentiment.'

The room was kitted out with two sofas that were facing each other. They were both navy blue, well worn but comfortable still. The padding of the seat moved around me as I dropped down opposite Fendley. I scanned the room for recording equipment and realised it must be neatly tucked away in a ceiling tile. There was low-budget artwork on the walls, throw cushions on the sofas and, when I scanned the room further, I spotted a clutter of children's toys half-hidden.

'We thought you might be more comfortable in here,' Fendley said, perhaps guessing at my observations. 'This space is a little more homely. Or we like to think it is, anyway. The interview rooms, they're for more... I don't know what word I'm looking for.' Another near-laugh that faded to a smile. 'Are you okay, Agnes?'

I recognised her tone. She spoke to me how she might speak to a child or another vulnerable person and then it– Knock-clicked into place: *Here, I'm a victim...*

Fendley did all the talking. Craw only took notes now and then, and gave me a sympathetic downturned smile whenever my voice cracked with feeling, which was something I was trying hard not to overdo. I told them how Eliah and I had been drawn to each other from the first introductions. It wasn't a relationship that we'd leave our marriages for, that much we both knew from the accidental first afternoon we'd spent together. But we also knew it was hard for either to resist the temptation of the other. I drew us with heart-eyed emojis and tongues hanging out, like all adulterers imagined their flings.

'It sounds like you had something special,' Fendley added.

I shrugged. 'I'm too old to use that word for feelings. But there was certainly a connection there. Fin and I, we get along fine, but sometimes you want more than fine, don't you?' I searched her face for a flicker of recognition. She struck me as the loyal type, and I couldn't decide whether this was something she'd know anything about – or whether she was more likely to be the cuckolded. 'When I found out about Eliah, I was so upset about the whole ordeal and I... I was trying so hard to keep my grief in proportion.' My voice wavered and even *I* wondered whether I might cry a little. 'It didn't occur to me until much later how strange it was for a man to be strangled. Don't you think?'

Fendley narrowed her eyes. 'What do you mean by that, exactly?'

'May I?' I gestured to my laptop alongside me and she nodded. It didn't take long for the machine to stir into life and when it did I clicked into the folder marked 'Research proposals'. Fin had never been interested in my work. I knew anything in this folder or similarly titled ones would be safe from prying eyes. Not that the contents mirrored the name. Inside, I double-clicked a video file that unfolded to reveal a dark room, two silhouettes – then I turned the screen to face them.

Out of my sight line, I only knew where the video was based on the grunt and huffs and– Knock. Knock.

'You want me to stop?' Fin's voice. 'Are you sure?'

Knock. I could remember him applying a shove of pressure before he eased his hand away. Air had rushed into me with the force of a punch, and when I took the glass of water he'd offered I soon spluttered out the shy sips I'd taken. Then the crackle of the footage came to an end.

'When was this?' Fendley asked. Her voice was harder than it had been before.

'Six months ago.'

'Consensual?'

I nodded. 'The knock, that's our safe gesture.'

'Like a safe word?' Craw asked and Fendley threw him a disapproving look.

'Exactly.' I stared hard at a spot on the floor to give myself a vacant look. 'Fin enjoys breath play. Once I'd told Eliah about it, he wanted to try it too and–'

'Eliah also choked you?' Fendley handed me the explanation.

'Yes.' There'd been no mention of the gym bag, stashed in a locker somewhere. To think I'd once fantasised about the accident of someone finding it. By now they must have done – and I'd finally explained it for them. 'He'd never done it before but once he started, he loved it. He was different to Fin, though, always...' I imagined tightening a brace around his throat. 'Gentler.'

'You and Fin have a different dynamic?'

I pointed to the laptop. 'If you back-click out of the folder, you'll find pictures.' I paused while she followed my instruction, and slowly I watched their faces change. 'He's done it on and off since we got married. Never before, oddly enough. There was one time... It was so bad after I could hardly speak for two days, and that's when I thought the pictures mightn't be a terrible idea. I didn't take pictures... I mean, that's not an exhaustive folder. It's just the worst of it. Which is unfair, really.'

Fendley huffed again. 'I wouldn't call it unfair, Agnes.'

'I only mean, not every time was like this.'

'But there were enough times for you to be concerned.'

I murmured my agreement. 'Like I said, I was so busy hiding my feelings about Eliah's death that... I don't know. I don't know what I'm trying to say here.' I let my breath shudder out of me as

I doubled over and set my elbows against my thighs, my head lolled between my knees. 'God, what am I doing here?'

The seat dipped next to me and I realised, then, that Fendley had moved to my sofa. She set a hand between my shoulder blades and I could feel the heat of her palm through my shirt. It was a comforting gesture and I wondered whether they'd trained her in that, or whether it was years of practice.

'You're alerting us to new lines of enquiry,' she said, her voice level. But then she spoke in a quieter tone, as though shutting Craw out of the conversation. 'You're doing the right thing in bringing this to us, Agnes, I promise you. It's the right thing for Eliah.'

I lifted my head in time for a single tear to roll out of me. 'What about Fin?'

Her face hardened then. 'You let us worry about him.'

CHAPTER EIGHTEEN

I magine making someone the angriest they've ever been. Then fusing them in a situation where they can do nothing about it.

Fendley and Craw warned me that their investigation would unveil the affair. But when I was faced with the option of telling Fin myself or having them beat me to the finish line, I decided to be the tortoise of the fable. When he came home early from work a day later, punctuating his arrival with a door slam so furious I worried it might shake the structure of the house, I knew that he knew. He soon huffed and puffed and blew–

'Is this marriage a fucking game to you, Agnes? A big fucking game?'

A big game would come with a big safe word. But he'd never told me a route out.

I stayed quiet while the spittle flew from his mouth; accusations and slurs rumbled up from the rough of his throat. He shouted with such a ferocity that I feared he might not have voice enough left in him to call his mistress and tell her what a deceitful bitch I was.

When he finished, he poured himself three fingers of Scotch and sat opposite me at the dining table. Wordlessly, he swallowed a greedy mouthful and slid the tumbler along the veneer surface to land by me. I took it as an instruction to drink. I was taking my own thirsty swig when he spoke again.

'How long?'

'Five months.'

'Fucking hell, Agnes.' He pulled the glass back. 'We'd only just settled here.'

'We'd been here for three months,' I answered, as though that were a defence. Then I added, 'And I think you'd been sleeping with Irene Loughty for a similar length of time by then. Or was it slightly longer?'

I chanced a look at him and found that he was staring at the honey of the glass.

He pulled in a long breath and then said, 'Agnes, that's beside the point.'

I thought it would be.

'What did the police tell you?'

'We're not talking about what the police told me. I want to know *your* version of events, from the beginning. Who made the first move?'

Eliah wasn't going to give evidence against me, at least, so I could afford to say what I wanted. 'He did.'

'Bastard. Where?'

'The evening we were having drinks at Xara's, all of us. You were—'

'Downstairs, playing the good husband and charming the arse off the wives.'

Fin had been suspicious at the time, I remembered, then. When we came home that evening he'd commented on how long it had taken me to navigate my way to the bathroom and back, and how flushed I'd been when I walked into the living room again. Eliah had already escaped, and I'd found him vaping out of an upstairs window. My discovery had been accidental though; I really had been trying to find the bathroom. But when I snatched the machine away from him, pulled in a drag of something that reminded me of birthday cake – baked with nicotine – I'd leaned forward to blow the fumes right into his mouth. I'd pulled him to me by the back of his head, kissed him hard and handed the machine back.

'He kissed me,' I said. 'Only once, and... I didn't kiss back that time. But I hadn't been able to stop thinking about it and...' I trailed off when he upended the contents of the tumbler into his mouth. 'You don't need to know this.'

He thudded the glass down. 'Don't tell me what I need.'

'Have you eaten?'

'Walk down memory lane given you an appetite?'

I shook my head and stood without an answer. 'I'm going to order food. What–'

'You dare ask me what I want.'

'Then don't be surprised if I get it wrong.'

Fin drank another tumbler of Scotch in the time it took for the delivery driver to arrive with egg noodles, steamed vegetables and diced meat. I found two complimentary fortune cookies in the bottom of the paper bag and I threw them in a drawer; it seemed unlikely that either of us could stand to know what might happen next. While I was serving food into bowls Fin loitered at the island. Alcohol always made him hungry and, given our circumstances then, I imagined he would feel especially irked that I knew him so well – and that I'd got his order right. He didn't say as much, but when he impatiently shovelled noodles into his mouth using only his fingers, it became clear that Chinese takeout, two drinks in, was the sweet spot, even while having a conversation about adultery. By the time he'd upgraded to using cutlery, he was talking to me like I was a human being again.

He forked a piece of chicken into his mouth and spoke around it, 'Are you unhappy? This life, the life that I've built for us, does it make you unhappy?'

I said nothing of his affair, then, nothing of my suspicions that it wasn't his first; nothing of the fact that this grand life he spoke of wasn't one that I asked for, either. I only dipped my head and addressed my answer to the food that I'd hardly touched. 'No, Fin, it doesn't make me unhappy.' I danced a cluster of noodles around my fork. 'Since I finished work, since we moved here, there have been times when I've felt–'

'Lonely. Unfulfilled.' He huffed. 'Don't be a cliché, Agnes.'

Says the man who's fucking his younger female colleague. 'I'm sorry.'

'What would you have done if you'd fallen pregnant?' he asked, and the subject change made my stomach lurch over. 'Were you being sensible at least?'

'We were always sensible, yes, I–'

'Did you even *want* to get pregnant?'

The quiet accusation inside the question made my eyes prick with feeling. I scooped a sprig of broccoli into my mouth and slow chewed for long enough to blink the emotion away, then I cleared my throat before I answered plainly, 'Yes.' I didn't know whether it was a lie, exactly. But I could easily remember the relief that I nursed like a thirty-week foetus full in the base of my gut, the last time I'd been greeted by the sight of bloodied underwear.

'Do you still want to get pregnant?'

I felt another lurch in me. 'Even after this?'

'You expect it to get in the way?'

No, but incarceration might. 'I... I don't know what I expect, Fin.'

He drained the last of another drink and bounced the empty tumbler in his palm. I recognised his deadpan stare from times in bed together. He pulled his arm back, then, as though about to launch the glass in my direction. When I didn't flinch at the threat, he lowered it back down. He couldn't afford to be seen scraping broken glass into the outdoor bin. My husband knew exactly how that would look.

'Does anyone know about the affair?'

'The police...'

He sighed. 'Anyone else, I mean, Agnes. Friends?'

I knew who he meant and no, I wasn't likely to admit to it. 'I didn't tell her.'

'I'm sure Violet would have encouraged the behaviour if you had.'

'She isn't the tart you think she is.'

'By your standards?' he snapped. He pushed the empty glass toward me and nodded, and I followed the implied instruction. 'The police asked about my whereabouts the afternoon Eliah was murdered,' he added, when I was facing away from him, and I was thankful he couldn't see my reaction. 'I told them we were together, here.'

'Did you tell them about your run?'

'And create a black hole in my timeline? Of course not. I told them we were here, together, all afternoon. We're both in the clear.'

I kept my head downturned to hide the echo of a smile as I walked back. He grabbed my hand before I could get to my own seat and pulled me close to him. The squeeze of him was too rough to be anything affectionate, even though his full eyes looked like they might brim over with tears when he stared up at me. He narrowed his gaze, peered inside me and behind every word I'd said as though looking for hairline fractures in the story so far.

'I'm telling you the truth about it all,' I said eventually.

He shook his head. 'I'll never know that, will I?' Then he let me go with a gentle shove in the direction of my own chair. He sipped the drink and winced. 'We won't part ways over this, Agnes, to be clear. But it's certainly going to be a difficult period for us going forwards, I need for you to understand that now.'

Love, you have no idea. I nodded in understanding.

'I assume you want to stay married to me?' he asked, though he didn't wait for an answer. 'I'd suggest counselling but... I don't like the thought of this getting out. Other people would have too much to say about it.'

I knew then that I had to tell the wives as soon as I could; it would be good character development, for myself and for Fin. 'I understand, Fin.'

'I think it's best if you sleep down here this evening. Some space might–' The thrum of my phone against the tabletop interrupted him. I didn't glance at the caller, but he leaned over to take a look. 'You should answer. It's Xara.'

'It won't be anything important.'

He lowered his drink from a more generous sip. 'It will be if she heard shouting.'

I snatched at the handset. 'Xara, I'm just in the middle of something, can I–'

'Agnes, no, I just *had* to call. Have you heard yet? About Nicole?'

'What about Nicole?' I glanced up at Fin, who looked notably tuned out from the conversation I was having. But I knew there was no real way he wasn't listening.

'Christ, Agnes, something has come undone with her first statement and... I don't know the details, but she's been pulled back in, for questioning.'

CHAPTER NINETEEN

Gathered around Jessa and Umi's firepit, I felt more like a recently initiated member of a coven than I ever had before – and that included the mock-up animal sacrifice I'd made of a Barbie in Mum's back garden, aged eight.

It was the evening after Fin and I had talked through the details of Eliah; although it had felt less like a talk and more like a thorough interview that put Fendley's skills to shame. Had the circumstances been different, I might have suggested Fin consider a career change, but it didn't seem like a comment he'd take with the intended whimsy.

When Xara had called that night, she told me Nicole had been pulled in for questioning 'under shady circumstances'. She didn't elaborate, and I didn't know whether it was tension building or whether she just hadn't had the time to magpie at the evidence. But she'd text soon after to suggest wine and whines at Jessa and Umi's so I thought there was gossip afoot, if not actual information to be shared.

'Why are you suddenly so close to them?' Fin had asked when I mentioned going.

Because it pays to be. 'Because I'm lonely.'

There'd been a long silence before he'd answered. 'Fine, go.'

Nothing more was said about my being out. Although he soon decided that he may as well be out himself if I weren't around. I murmured my agreement and swallowed the salt-bitter urge to ask him if he wouldn't mind giving my best to Irene.

I'd expected to see him before I left for drinks, but Fin didn't come home from work that evening. While I got ready for my night across the road, I imagined him and Irene leaving work together. Did everyone know? I wondered. Did they leave, hand in hand, without a care for who might see them? The thought had caused such a turn in me that I had to put a pause on applying my eyeliner for fear that I'd blind myself. My grandmother might have said that would be an eye for an eye. When my hand was steady again, I restarted in drawing my face on but I still couldn't shake the wonder – not of what they were doing, only who knew they were doing it. Was that the type of housewife I was? The one spoken of in hushed tones, pity-laden, with former colleagues questioning how I could possibly not know what my husband was–

'Agnes, are you okay?'

The thoughts had followed me from front door to front door, and I'd missed much of the conversation about holidays, diets and what everyone thought of the quiche.

'I'm sorry, I've been away with the fairies all day. Has anyone heard from Nicole?' I leaned across to take another triangle from the plate of prepared food that sat between me and Jessa. Umi had made quiche from Nicole's recipe; a homage to the fallen woman. It was tasteless but at least it kept my mouth busy.

'I wondered when we'd get on to that.' Jessa sat forward and spread her palms in front of the open flames. 'Xara, you're more in the loop about this, surely.'

'I didn't want to go right into the gossip part of the evening,' Xara lied. A lick of colour spread up her face as she spoke, and I decided she must be terrible at poker. 'I don't know what the latest news is, from today, I mean, but I can tell you as much as I know from her being pulled in.'

'Who's your source?' Umi asked, eyebrow arched. She was an editor by trade and the eye for detail followed her everywhere.

Xara rolled her eyes. 'Who do you think?'

'Fine, fine, a trusted informant, go ahead.'

Xara was about to launch into an explanation, but I cut her off. 'Wait, I'm sorry–'

'I keep forgetting you're new here,' Umi spoke over me. I looked across and she winked. 'Yeah, Xara, who's your source?' She sounded more playful, then.

'Look, it's nothing. But I have this old boyfriend–'

'Who Dermot doesn't know about,' Jessa added.

'Yes, okay, whatever. Who Dermot doesn't know about. He's a uniform officer, that's all, but he's got a good ear on the ground for the occasional bit of idle gossip. He reached out years ago when we had a load of burglaries in the villages. You remember, don't you?' Jessa and Umi mumbled in agreement; it was another thing that existed here before me; that hadn't been spoken of when we were asking questions about the area. 'Anyway, he reached out then, and we've sort of just kept in touch.'

'But Dermot doesn't know,' Umi underscored.

Xara reached over to tap her thigh in reproach. 'I think Agnes has got the idea that Dermot doesn't know, thanks all the same.'

They're all hiding their little secrets. I smiled. 'Is there anything for him to know?'

She shook her head. 'There really isn't. We're just good

friends and it was a hundred years ago when anything last happened with us.' She paused to sip her wine and I wondered whether it was strategic. 'Dermot and I are happily married. Luke is happily still playing the field. That's all there is to say about that.'

But I didn't buy it. There was the same flash of colour on her face as before.

'That's all there is to say,' Umi parroted. 'But she still won't tell her husband.' She stood, then, and kissed Jessa on the crown of her head. 'I'm going indoors for supplies. Don't start the idle gossip without me.'

In Umi's absence, Jessa teased Xara further about her own non-affair. I didn't have her written as the disloyal type. Nor did she strike me as a sexual enough person to suffer from the affliction of simply not being able to keep her hands off someone. I'd seen her and Dermot together through their living room window enough times to know they were the archetype married couple who had sex at set times, then brushed their teeth together over matching sinks before going to bed. The thought caused a cramp in my gut. But there was a notable change in her all the same at further mentions of Luke; a change that said perhaps nothing had happened, but the mind did wander.

'Thank God for that,' Xara said when Umi made a return. 'Your wife is roasting me here and poor Agnes doesn't know what to make of it all.'

I laughed. 'I didn't have you down as the type that might— Umi, what is that?'

She exhaled a plume of smoke. 'You're not morally opposed, are you?'

Jessa took the joint from her wife. 'If so, you don't have to have any.'

Who the hell are *these women?*

127

'Xara, are you smoking that?' I asked her, in what I hoped was a neutral tone.

'I am, once I've told you all about Nicole. I need a level head for this.' She shifted around in her seat, pulled her blanket up to her chin and said, 'Her alibi has fallen through.' Jessa choked on an inhale of smoke but Xara wasn't put off. 'By all accounts, she *was* at the charity event, and initially there was a shedload of people who were happy to verify she was there. There were even *pictures* of her there, for God's sake. But when some sneaky detective nosed about further, she pulled up footage of Nicole's car leaving the multistorey earlier than she'd told them she had. And after that there's no sign of her going back to the party.' She leaned forward and plucked the cigarette-with-extras from Umi. 'What do you make of that?'

I skimmed back to the conversation from weeks earlier: Nicole mentioning feelings for someone else. *But she wouldn't have, would she?*

'Well, bugger me,' Jessa answered.

'Later,' Umi replied without missing a beat, and Jessa slapped her arm.

'Agnes, care for a try?'

I hadn't smoked cannabis since I was sixteen years old. I couldn't remember being particularly impressed by it then. But under the peer pressure of being a valued member of the housewife community, I snatched the offered joint and took a generous pull on it.

'I can't believe she doesn't have an alibi.' Smoke fell out of me at the same time as the words did. 'Do they think she did it?'

'Jesus.' Umi was staring into the fire. 'I didn't think of Nicole as—'

'Easy, drama,' Jessa interrupted. 'Don't think of her as anything yet, other than a friend who's recently lost her husband.'

'In suspicious circumstances,' Xara added, and when I looked at her I caught a smirk. The weed had already brought out something more mischievous in her.

'Your boyfriend doesn't know whether she's a real suspect or...' Jessa started.

'He isn't my boyfriend, and no. But he'll call when he knows more, he said.'

'I'll bet he will.'

I saw everyone in a different shade. Xara was cheeky; Jessa was flirty; Umi was staring into the firepit like there was a showreel of her predicted future in there. And I was desperate to be liked by them all – which made me wonder whether the joint was less of a joint and more a time machine.

In the needy tone of my sixteen-year-self, I said, 'I have a secret.'

Umi's head snapped up. 'It wasn't you, was it?'

'What?' I thought my heart might thump through me.

'Ignore her,' Jessa intervened. 'The weed makes her twitchy.' She leaned forward in her bucket seat so she could reach over and grab my hand. 'We all have secrets, Agnes, don't worry.'

'Am I the only one who needs a follow-up on what the secret is though?' Xara said, and laughed. 'I mean, you don't *have* to tell us. But we are excellent at keeping secrets.'

I smiled. I believed her. 'I was sleeping with Eliah.' The words fell out followed by what I thought was a string of dribble, but when I reached up to wipe my chin there was nothing there. 'Fin knows, so do the police,' I rushed to add.

'Does Nicole?'

'Do you have an alibi?'

'Yes, she does,' Umi answered Xara's question before I could think to.

Instead, I answered Jessa's. 'I don't know whether Nicole knows.'

And then, in a display that I hadn't expected from a coven of half-baked housewives, they flocked to me with sympathies. Jessa disappeared to get more wine while Umi crossed to my side of the pit and hunched over me from behind. She draped her arms around my shoulders.

'God, to think we were just over the road when it was happening,' she said, then kissed my crown in the same way she had done Jessa's earlier in the night.

Meanwhile, Xara dropped to her knees in front of me. The cheeky tones were dormant. She only grabbed both hands, then, and shifted about like a watercolour until she finally settled in my eyeline. 'We're all in this together, Agnes, all of us. We're a troop, us women.'

I felt Umi nod. 'A faction, that's what we are.'

CHAPTER TWENTY

The days after that were uneventful and I was glad of it. The excitement that the wives had shown in light of the affair was shocking. But they weren't judgemental; only intrigued. How long had it been happening, they wanted to know, and how long had Fin known? It was Jessa who asked the Big Money question, sheepishly with atmospheric flames rising between us: 'Did Fin already know when Eliah was murdered, or has he found out since?' She and I shared a look as I carefully explained I had told him since – not that he didn't know – and I hoped she noted my phrasing.

In the morning after, during a tense breakfast time together, when Fin had asked how the evening had gone I gave him minimal details: enough to denote enjoyment but not enough to warrant suspicion, which I could already see radiating out from him in cartoon heatwaves.

When the front doorbell rang and cut through the sour core of our breakfast, we both stood and rushed. I realised, then, we were each as desperate as the other for an excuse to leave. But Fin beat me to the hall and I only lingered in the doorway while he saw to whoever the visitor was.

Jessa was fidgeting on the threshold to the house. Her head snapped round and her eyes shot wide with surprise when she saw Fin waiting. 'Oh.'

'Jessa, always a pleasure,' he said, with a charm I imagined he must reserve for the women in his workplace – or the men, if he was trying to win funding for something. 'What can we do for you on this fine morning?'

The sky outside was grey with a threat of rain.

She fidgeted again, danced from one foot to the other. 'I wasn't expecting you, Finian, I was actually here for Agnes, if she's...' She craned to one side to get a clearer look at me. 'Are you well, Agnes?'

I'd never seen her so awkward. 'Yes, thanks, Jessa, *are you?*'

'I was actually hoping to grab some advice from you.' I could tell she was lying from the high creep in her voice and I wondered whether Fin had caught sound of it, too. 'Fancy a walk?' She made a show of looking around her. 'Before this fine morning turns into a wet one?'

Fin laughed. 'Perhaps I overstated the weather conditions for us. Either way, lovely to see you, Jessa.' He turned and padded back towards me. His insincere smile was still fixed in place when he came to a stop and kissed my cheek. 'Take care, sweetheart, especially of that weather turning.'

'Thank you, darling. I'll be fine.'

I walked to meet Jessa, and grabbed a coat from the stand on my way through. When the door was firmly shut behind me I snatched at her hand.

'What on earth is wrong?'

A nervous laugh crept out of her. 'Nothing, Agnes. God, I am sorry. Fin just caught me by surprise, opening the door like that.'

Mad, how people will go ahead and do that, when the doorbell rings. But she looked too unnerved for a snide comeback, so I only said, 'He isn't working today so we can spend some time together, that's all.'

'That's really lovely, Agnes, honestly. Especially after everything you said.' She paused as though considering the situation in more detail, then rushed to add, 'Oh bugger, and I've gone ahead and pulled you away fr–'

'Really, Jessa, it's fine.' It was my turn to shift awkwardly then. I side-eyed her while we trod the garden track and walked towards the nearest public footpath: the one I'd taken a run along the day Eliah was murdered, that is. But that wasn't a thing to be nervous over. Although nothing more had been said about the wives' misspent time together – with a joint and six bottles of wine shared four ways – I couldn't deny that there were certain parts of the evening I'd misplaced, no matter the searching. Now, faced with the threat of 'everything you said', I wondered whether my mouth had run off without me somewhere between bottle five and six.

'I'm a bit nervous,' I admitted. 'Some of what I said has slipped down the cracks.'

She laughed. 'I think we all feel a bit like that.' She reached to wrap an arm around my shoulders, side on still, and squeezed. 'You didn't say anything to worry about, though, and certainly nothing that we won't keep to ourselves.' Another squeeze. 'We're a team, us women.'

It sounded like she meant it, which made me all the more curious – and concerned – about what had brought her outside my front door. She dropped her arm to her side, then tucked her hands into her pockets and pulled in a deep breath. It sounded like the precursor to more speech, yet she stayed silent for a while. Everything in me wanted to accelerate whatever this was. But the nerves of her in the face of Fin also left me wondering whether it was a better tactic not to startle her.

'Shall we?' she said. She'd been so quiet up to that point that the sound nearly startled me. When I looked up and around, at the bench she was gesturing to, I realised we were halfway along the walk that Fin/I had ran along. Another few minutes on the track and we'd find the point where we fell.

'Please. For a runner, I'm lacking in energy today.'

She laughed and took a seat. 'Umi mentioned you were a runner. Often?'

I groaned. 'Not as often as I should. This is one of my routes, actually.'

'Oh, lovely.' She looked around. 'Lovely.'

Her hands dropped into her lap and she made a loose cat's cradle with her fingers, knotting them and unknotting, knotting and–

'Not to sound suspicious.' I reached across and set one hand over both of hers. 'But something doesn't feel quite right here. Are you okay, Jess?'

Jessa looked at me with eyes that were full of feeling. I worried she was so close to spilling emotion on me that I considered moving away from her, to try to miss any stray splashes. But pulling my hand away didn't feel like a supportive gesture. Instead, I only squeezed and flashed her a thin smile which I hoped might look encouraging. She squeezed back, and then looked out at the view ahead of us. It would have been a beautiful sight, if my concentration hadn't been split between two uncomfortable strands: being accused of murder, which was an undying concern now; or Jessa *actually* having a personal problem that she thought I was friend enough to help with. There was a stand-off in me as to which possibility was worse. Though of course I knew friendship with her couldn't be *that* bad.

'Agnes, something has happened, and I'm torn between the right thing and the... I don't know, the thing a friend might do, or the thing someone loyal might do. Do you know the sort of worry I mean?'

I huffed. 'Boy, do I.' *No, no I do not.*

'The problem is, Agnes, it's about something... or someone, rather, more about someone who lives in the village, and I'm just not sure...' She shook her head and whatever the end of the sentence was it died in her before it made its way out. 'Would you want to know?' she asked, then.

It felt like an unfair question; only half of the necessary mixture had been added, so I couldn't get a reasonable taste for it. Still, it was obvious that Jessa was nursing something too heavy for her to carry alone, and I found myself pulled into another two strands of thought: *it's either about me, and I need to defuse this; or it's about someone else, and I need to use it.*

I shuffled along to close the gap between us and pulled her into a half-hug. When she relaxed into me, I said, 'I think I'd want to know.'

In my peripheral vision I saw her nod, but her stare stayed fixed ahead.

'I saw Fin on the day Eliah was murdered.'

A surge of something warm rushed through my belly and I shot away from her like our close contact was directly responsible for it. From the worried look of her, I thought it was probably an appropriate response to what she was implying, too. 'Okay. Well, Fin lives in the village.' I forced a laugh. 'He's allowed to have been in the village the same day that Eliah...'

She shook her head. 'He was pretty beaten up, Agnes.'

'I don't... I don't think I understand.'

But of course I understood: Fin had taken his fall. When he'd walked into the kitchen that day, he'd looked like someone who'd been in the wars – or at a crime scene.

'I'm not accusing or implying or...' She reached for me, then,

135

but she held her palm up and waited for me to close the distance to her. When my cold hand was clamped against the warmth of hers she asked, 'Did you see him, when he came home that day?' But she cut me off with a follow-up before I could pretend to struggle my way through an answer. 'I'm not accusing him of anything, Agnes, or you. I... I understand. I *would* understand, if you'd seen him that day and if you didn't know what to do or how to approach things. I'd get it. What I'm saying is...' She paused for a swallow so severe that I heard the glug of it. 'What I'm saying is the police are coming to do follow-up interviews soon, about Nicole, I think, and I have to decide whether I mention this, which I *know* in my tummy is the right thing. But, God, we're just so close now, Agnes.'

My head shot up. *So it* does *pay to be close.* 'What are you saying?'

She formed an O with her lips and forced out a long breath. 'I'm saying that if Umi were Fin, and you were me then I'd want to know. But I don't know that I'd want you to tell the police.'

'Okay.' I counted to five, to create the illusion of putting some thought into the matter, and then I answered, 'I don't want you to tell the police.'

She squeezed my knee, then, and stood. 'Then I won't. Shall we head back?'

'Wait.' I jumped up and set a hand on her arm to stop her from moving off. 'That's it? There's no more to say about it?'

'There's no more to say about it.' She half-laughed and started to move away from me. 'I told you, Agnes,' she spoke over her shoulder, 'we're all a team now.'

CHAPTER TWENTY-ONE

In the days after, Fin had taken two phone calls, in the house but in a separate room. He'd tried to excuse himself discreetly, like I wouldn't notice the muffled sound of his voice elsewhere in the house, only seconds after his exit. But it was clear enough what was happening. I wagered Irene was becoming excitable, demanding more of his time. If that were the case, I wagered it wasn't long before he finished things with her. Fin had never cared for women that he didn't have to chase and change.

On the afternoon of the second phone call, he crept back into the kitchen like nothing had happened. I was sitting at the table which was decorated with open catalogues: wallpaper prints, sofas and pop-up partition walls that could change the feel of the space. In being a housewife with no children to tend, I'd found this was one of many tricks that disguise a restless woman as a busy one. I didn't even look up when he came in, only licked my finger and flicked a page.

'Are we redecorating?' He stood over me.

'Oh, I don't know.' I looked up; an angle I knew he liked.

'Don't you sometimes just want a change about the place?' I tried for the most dulcet tones I could muster.

'I quite like this.' He leaned forward and tapped a wallpaper print that was busy enough to induce a migraine, but I gasped all the same.

'That's the one I've been eyeing up, too.'

He kissed the crown of my head. 'You always did have impeccable taste, sweetheart. Where were you thinking?' He moved behind me, then, and set a hand on either shoulder. The way he kneaded at the skin made me think of Eliah.

'That's the one thing I'm not sure of.'

'How about the spare room?'

I clicked my fingers. 'Excellent.' I reached forward to dog-ear the page over. 'I'll keep that safe and add it to the purchase list before I send any orders off. Do you want me to wait, Fin, and we can look through things together?'

Another kiss to the crown before he moved away. 'You have a good time with it, sweetheart, busy yourself. Let me know how much it'll be before you order? I wouldn't want anything to query on the card bill when I get it.' He was shrugging on his coat by the close of his sentence. 'You'll be okay for a while, while I'm out?'

'I didn't realise you were out today.' There was a long silence, then, and I wondered whether I'd stepped too far in challenging him. Over the last week we'd shifted gears dramatically: he from scorned husband to adoring one; me from manipulative wife to suspicious one. I couldn't understand how he'd swept Eliah to one side quite so neatly. But from the look on his face, I thought this one comment might be the thing to bring it all spilling out.

'Work,' he answered plainly, and that was all the bite I got from him. 'You'll be in this evening, not out with your new friends?' He didn't sound playful.

'I'll be here, waiting, browsing catalogues.' My face was still buried between pages. 'Drive safe, and I'll see you later.'

I saw him cross the space again and then he lowered himself well enough to kiss my cheek. 'I love you, Agnes.'

And the sincerity of it made me guess something was wrong.

The sun was high enough for me to sit in the last of its warmth. I'd spent most of the afternoon in the garden, alternating between the social media feeds of the wives. I couldn't fathom what they did all day but there was obviously enough happening to keep them busy, and I rolled their enough-ness around my mouth like bitter fruit. I didn't want to call any of them for fear of seeming as needy as I felt, so instead I settled for idle scrolling. But when I stumbled across Nicole's feed my interest flickered into something more lively. There was a stream of sympathetic posts dating back from the days after Eliah's death. In the recent days, though, there looked to have been very little posted. And I wondered whether news of her questioning – of the alibi that held water like an old sieve – had found its way to the masses. I'd deliberately avoided media outlets as a source on it all in case I scared myself half to confession, but I felt a deep ache then to know what the newspapers might be saying about her. The hapless housewife with a husband strangled to death in the upstairs of their neat cottage? The headlines wrote themselves.

I was a finger shift away from clicking on Eliah's profile when my phone hummed to life.

'I was about to do something terrible,' I answered. 'Thanks for calling.'

139

'Are you with Fin?' There was a horrible worry in Vi's voice that didn't suit her. 'Or anyone, for that matter.'

'I'm home alone. Are you okay? Did something happen?'

She puffed. 'No and yes. Look, I'm about to tell you something, Agnes, and I don't know what I expect you to do with this information necessarily, because frankly there's not a lot you can do. But you need to know.'

'Christ, Vi, you don't usually go in for the dramatics. What's–'

'You'll understand when I explain but... Agnes, don't do anything rash.'

I didn't answer, because it felt like an unfair ask. But she pushed.

'Promise me.'

'Fine, I promise,' I agreed, sounding every bit as petulant as I felt. 'What's happened?'

'I have a colleague who–'

'You're sleeping with?' I interrupted.

She hesitated before she answered, 'Yes, but that's not the story for this particular conversation. I have a colleague who I'm sleeping with, which is why he felt he could come to me with this. But it's career-ruining stuff.' Her speech was littered with pauses. I imagined her pacing her office, hand clamped to her forehead, suffering a frantic back and forth on whether to tell me. But Vi was strong-headed. If she'd got far enough through her thinking to decide on a phone call, she'd already decided to go through with whatever this was. So I sucked in my platitudes and let her grapple with her conscience between sentences. 'The work friend is a psychologist in the office two doors down. He also deals with private patients, exclusively, and recently he was contacted by a man voicing concerns for his wife.' There was a long pause, littered with muttered expletives under her breath that I thought I perhaps wasn't meant to hear. 'It's Fin, Agnes. The man who's concerned about his wife, it's *your* Fin.'

There was a ferocious buzzing around me. I couldn't work out whether Vi kept talking in the seconds after the reveal – or whether the conversation was paused for a swarm of bees to descend around my ears. I leaned forward, elbows on knees, and tried to deep breathe into the handset.

'You need to hold your out-breath for a second longer,' Vi said and I realised the buzzing must be clearing. 'That's it,' she said when I followed instructions. 'Good girl, Agnes, just a second or two longer.'

I managed to right myself then. 'How did you... I mean, how did that even...'

'He, the man I'm involved with, he's heard me mention your name. In passing conversation I must have mentioned Fin's and... I can't lie, Agnes, I've mentioned Fin in an unfavourable light once or twice. From what I've said about you, and from what I imagine Fin must have said about you, it wasn't adding up. So he, the man, that is—'

'Does he have a name?' I snapped. My normal faculties were unfolding.

'Not one that I'm prepared to share. I'm not getting him struck off for this.'

'I'd be more likely to send him a bottle of something in thanks.'

She half-laughed. 'There you are.'

I trod back through the double doors and into the kitchen. It was a socially acceptable hour for drinking long before this phone call; I reasoned that in the midst of it, I was entitled to swill the news down with a glass of something full-bodied.

'Are you drinking?' she asked, just as the first explosion of colour hit the base of my glass.

'I will be in a second.'

'That won't help.'

'It won't hinder. What else do you know?'

She sighed. 'I know Fin has been reporting back some unsavoury behaviours. Times when you can't remember things you've said or done. Conversations you've been having by yourself, that have suddenly stopped when he's entered the room. There have been one or two things you've been convinced are true, even when faced with evidence they aren't, and... Agnes, there's a whole bloody list of things and none of it's you, I know it isn't. But they are signs that would cause a doctor or specialist to advise–'

'Intervention.'

There was a long pause during which I could hear the shake of her breath. 'What the fuck is happening between the two of you?'

I swallowed a greedy mouthful of wine. 'He knows about Eliah. This is my punishment, isn't it?'

'Agnes, come on. You don't think–'

'You know as well as I do, a woman who expresses a greater sexual desire than her male partner might express, the only logical conclusion is to have her locked up. It's a reasonable response.' My tone was flat; I felt like someone had let the air out of me.

'You think that's what this is over?'

That, or he knows what I did...

'That's madness, Agnes.'

I let out a curt laugh. 'That's what he's accusing me of for crossing him, Vi, absolute madness, don't you think? He's trying to convince that nameless man friend of yours that I'm some kind of crazy woman.'

I tipped my head back, drained my glass and slammed it down on the counter.

I'll show him crazy.

CHAPTER TWENTY-TWO

F in never did have a head for dates. Dad's birthday rolled around quietly. On the morning when he asked what my plans were for the day, I only said I was planning a trip out of the village but that I wasn't sure yet where I'd end up. He hadn't been paying enough attention to push. After he'd left I got ready in silence. The sound of Xara shouting from across the road as I was leaving – 'Morning, Agnes!' – was enough to make me jump. I only waved back, climbed into the car and continued the quiet on the way to the florist.

'Roses, please, white, a dozen of them,' I ordered from the woman behind the counter and phased out her chatter while she tended and tied and– 'I'm sorry, what?'

She laughed. 'I said to have a good day.'

The roses lay on the counter between us. I realised, then, that I'd scanned my card without even noticing. And I wondered whether this kind of disassociation had made it onto Fin's list of diagnostic criteria for the woman in the attic he was making me out to be. I thanked the florist and took the flowers back to the car, dropped them on the passenger seat and resisted the urge to strap them in. Their paper crackled as I rounded corners and braked sharply. They were the only noise accompaniment on the way to the graveyard. When I pulled into a parking space with an abrupt stop, the flowers flew from the seat and landed in the footwell.

'Sorry, Dad,' I said in a whisper as I leaned over to get them.

My mobile was balanced in a cup-holder next to me and I wondered who I could call to report the crushing weight in my belly. The knot of feelings was so uncomfortable that I thought I might be about to bleed. *But I'm a week early if I am.*

I unlocked the screen and clicked into my most recent calls: Xara; Jessa; Jessa; Xara; Umi; Vi. Since she lifted a veil on Fin's plans – or a partial veil, at least, given that I still didn't understand his endgame – Vi had called me every day to make sure I hadn't actually gone crazy. I sighed. *But who's to say I haven't?* I knew I could call her if I needed to and yet, my thumb hovered over her name with a horrible resistance to hitting dial. Instead, I clicked out of the calls and into my messages; the most recent was from Fin. He'd taken to texting throughout the day, mostly to ask what I was up to, which I took to be a guarded way of asking where I was and whether I was mid-coitus. I guessed that calls would interfere too much with his timetable; assuming that shagging Irene had been integrated into his Workload Allocation outline for the academic year. And with that thought of her, any thoughts I had at all about texting him withered away. He wasn't the person to lean on.

I locked the car, pocketed my keys and trod through the mud of the walkway towards the headstones. There must have been so much foot traffic through a graveyard on the average day; it had never occurred to me before. But the further I got along the path the less grubby it became, and it tweaked a sadness in me to think Dad was buried in the plots that were already long forgotten by relatives, hardly visited. It was the first time I'd visited him, though, and that only seemed to add credence to my worries.

The woman who'd arranged his funeral – the same woman who'd called to softly deliver the news of his death – had told me where his plot was, in case I wanted to visit. She'd afforded a similar consideration in the weeks before he died, too, a phone call to let me know how bad things were getting, in case I'd wanted to visit. I hadn't, but I didn't regret it either. I could see him now, I reasoned, and this was likely a close enough proximity to ensure that for the first time in maybe two decades we stood a chance of getting along.

The woman who had called me about the worsening condition, about the death, about the funeral; I hadn't even returned her last phone call. She only ever seemed to call with dreadful news, and after Dad dying I perished the thought at what else she might be calling to tell me. But there were times when I put some consideration into her. Gail hadn't told me that she was his partner, but she hadn't told me she was a care home attendant or nurse either. He and I hadn't been close enough for me to know the inner workings of his life. For all I knew, he might have been planning to stay with Gail for as long as he'd managed to stick it out with Mum. They could have been very happy together, living in a cottage with a thatched roof and open fire, with a sleepy spaniel napping in front of it, and at least one grandchild from Gail's daughter from her first marriage–

By the time I arrived at the right path to him, I'd imagined an entire life lived without me. I had to remind myself that that had been my choice.

I crouched down to set the flowers in front of him. Before I stood, I ran my fingertips over the indents of his name on the headstone. He'd had deep-set wrinkles in his face by the time my childhood hit; I could remember reading his expressions when I was sitting on his lap and Mum was shouting and–

I shook the rest of it away and exhaled a stream of cool air to steady myself.

'I was beat-up when I heard he'd passed.'

The voice came from too close behind me and I jolted.

'Oh, Christ, I'm sorry, I– Say, you're not little Agnes?'

There was a time when I would have corrected any man referring to me as 'little', but I let it go. It wasn't a hill to die on. Instead I held out a hand and smiled. 'Agnes, yes. I'm sorry, I...'

'Ah, you wouldn't remember me.' He shook my hand and waved away my concern with his free one. 'I was a friend of your dad's from the factory, way back when. I haven't seen you since you were about so high.' He measured up to his hip, but it didn't mean anything to me in terms of age. He took his cap off, then, and dipped his head. 'I really was sorry to hear about your dad. Cancer, they said?'

I nodded. 'They didn't catch it until quite late.'

'No, a few of the others, at the pub, that is, they said the same. Crying shame in this day and age, isn't it?' A long silence passed between us where I wondered what I was meant to say or do. I hadn't grieved in front of anyone before and the quiet expectation of it made me uncomfortable. He flashed a thin smile. 'My wife is a couple of rows over.' He pointed. 'I lost her to cancer about five years back now.'

At least I had a script for that. 'I'm so sorry to hear it.'

He shrugged. 'It happens. Life keeps rolling, doesn't it? But look here, I haven't even told you, I'm Noah.' He held out his hand again as though we hadn't already done this part. Still, I matched the gesture. 'It's funny, it's only a week or so ago I saw your mum up this way. I hadn't seen her in a long time either.'

No, neither have I. My stomach dropped. *I didn't even realise she was out.*

'The circumstances are dreadful, Agnes, but it's nice seeing you, kid. It's good to see you turned out right.'

I couldn't shake off his phrasing. It made me wonder how much he knew. But I only answered, 'It's been nice seeing you, Noah, circumstances aside and all. You take care now, won't you?'

I was already turning around when he said, 'Say hello to your old dear for me.'

Heat pricked the inside corners of my eyes and I felt two bulbs of feeling form. With one tight blink I sent them rushing down my cheeks, and I promised myself that that was the only show I was allowed. After that, I set about tidying up Dad's grave. I brushed away detritus from the top of the stone and used my glove to polish around his lettering, birth and death. There were stray leaves on the ground that I kicked over to the neighbours', just like I would have done as a child, and I imagined the reprimand I would have got for it.

I tapped the stone with the palm of my hand. 'No telling me off anymore, though, is there? Not for either of you.'

When the space was as respectable as a grave can be, I set a single kiss against his name and moved away. The walk back to the car seemed shorter than the one to the headstone and I wondered whether that was because I knew my way around the place now. It would be easier to find him the next time, I reasoned, assuming there was a next time at all. We hadn't been on good terms before, and it hardly seemed worth trying to pretend otherwise. The same couldn't be said of Mum, though; there might be good reason to pretend there. We hadn't been on talking terms for much of my marriage, but with her shady history she would make a better ally than she would a character witness against me: 'No, Agnes has never shown signs of poor mental health... Yes, a very stable upbringing.' Mum who had been in and out of rehabilitation centres for as long as I could remember. Mum who had been collecting convictions for minor offences since I was an early teen. Mum who had once said, 'I'll kill your father one day.' And I remember my young adult-self believing she truly meant it.

When I was back in the car, I reached across to pull my vape out of the glovebox. I inhaled hard, tipped my head back against the rest, and then exhaled candy cane sweetness through the top of my open window. Fin would guess it was perfume. I took four long drags of nicotine before I checked the time on my phone and found a text from Vi and a missed called from a withheld number. There was a voicemail, too.

I inhaled from the machine again and hit the key to connect to my service provider.

'You have one new message...'

The vape crackled as I breathed.

'Dr Villin, Agnes, it's Irene, Dr... I'm Dr Loughty, from work, with your husband. This is... I'm so sorry, this is difficult news and I'm sorry to tell you but Fin asked that I call. He said you'd know what to do. The police, they came a little while ago with questions and...'

I smiled. Dr Loughty's lectures must be a *blast* if her performance under pressure was anything to go by.

'They've taken him to the station for further questioning and I don't know... I don't know anything about his legal representation. He said he'd need some and... He said he needed you...'

Which I imagine must have been hard for you to hear, Irene.

I deleted the voicemail before listening to the end of it. Instead, I pulled up a fresh text message – "Thank you. xx" – and thumbed down to Jessa's number. When the swoosh sound indicated it had sent, I pocketed the handset and put my vape away. Then I took my sweet time in driving home to my empty, quiet house.

BEFORE

'Do you never get lonely, living in this place?'

He looked around the living room. 'What makes you ask?'

'It's just so quiet all the time.'

'I like my quiet.' He sat on the floor, opposite where I was posted on the sofa, and I guessed he wanted a full-frontal reaction to whatever was in the box. He handed it over with the smugness of a naughty child – or a cat bringing home a dead offering. 'Besides, it means I can make noise without worrying.'

I knew what he meant. 'You can just settle for normal loud sex with women, you know, you don't have to–'

'I don't have to *settle* for *normal* anything, that's what I know.' He squeezed my knee. 'I've been looking forward to this all week; let's not ruin it?'

I smiled and dipped my head in agreement. I'd been avoiding him, and although he wasn't the type to outright accuse me of having done that, I also knew he wasn't stupid enough not to have realised that's what I'd been doing either. The behaviour – his behaviour – had been escalating over the weeks into months that we'd been seeing each other. I'd encouraged it, too, that much I knew.

Whenever Dad called me with an update of home, I soon came here and thrashed and growled and – purged. That's what I was doing with him now; purging myself of the badness. Though I couldn't decide whether he was doing the same; or whether this just was his character. How any one person could enjoy hurting themselves – or being hurt – quite as much as he seemed to still felt alien, though, and the ways in which he pushed me – 'Come on, Agnes, you can be better than that.' – were only adding to my alienation from it all.

When I felt like that, though, there were perks to being far away from myself.

'Agnes, are you with me?' He cupped my knee and gently shook. 'Where did you go? You looked a million miles away.'

I tried to laugh. 'It's been a long week.'

'I could tell.' I narrowed my eyes at him, and he smiled. 'It's never been quite so hard to get a session out of you. I had no idea you were being worked quite so much.'

'Jealous?' I took on a softer tone and forced myself to be playful. I didn't want to steer this into an honest conversation if it could be avoided – and they could *always* be avoided, I had learned.

'Should I be?'

I leaned forward and kissed his cheek. 'Always. I'm in high demand.'

'I don't doubt it.' He nudged the box. 'But maybe this will keep your interest here.'

I couldn't delay it any longer, then, so I lifted the lid and– Something turned over in my stomach, chest, throat. I swallowed hard and tried to steady my breathing. He'd mentioned this once or twice before, but we'd never agreed on anything. Now it was here in front of me – all faux leather, buckles and cold metal – and I didn't know what reaction he wanted: schoolgirl glee; excited lover; killer inst–

He reached in and brought it out like a soft creature and said, 'It's easier than using your hand.'

CHAPTER TWENTY-THREE

P atrick was an old friend of Fin's; not mine. The two of them went back years. But despite their alleged closeness, Patrick hadn't been the best man at our wedding – hell, hadn't even been *at* the wedding when the time came, on account of a better offer on the day. The two seldom saw each other, that I knew of at least, but during the early days of mine and Fin's relationship when I saw them ready for boys' nights out or in, their relationship struck me as one loaded with secrets. I don't mean the who held whose hair out of the way while upchucking kind of secret, either. Their closeness came from something deeper than embarrassments and alcohol poisoning. It was an old boys' club friendship that I sensed ran deep enough to cater to illegalities if necessary. So Patrick was the perfect person to call to defend my darling husband.

Fin had been in custody for nearly twelve hours when the front doorbell rang out.

'Agnes, always a pleasure.' Patrick pushed in, kissed me on the cheek and powered through to the kitchen. I thought I heard him unclip his briefcase before I'd even got the front door closed. 'I'll take a coffee if you're making one.' I wasn't, but it seemed petty to make a thing of it. 'The shit they serve you in police stations gets worse by the day, honestly.'

I wandered in to join him. 'I'm surprised they don't have a Costa franchise there by now. Think of the money they'd make. Sugar?'

'Pardon?' His head snapped up. 'Oh. Oh, no, thank you.' He was rifling through papers and mumbling to himself. 'I'm right in thinking that you and Fin weren't together at the time the incident across the road took place.'

I turned to face him, folded my arms and waited for more.

'Is that correct?' he added, when the boil of the water became a percussion to our quiet.

'Yes, you're right in thinking that. But Fin told them otherwise.'

'Ah, so you know that part already.'

'He told me himself. When they interviewed him, and he found out about the affair.' I had gone back and forth on whether to be the one to mention it or not. But I eventually decided I'd rather pull the pin out on my own terms. 'He told them during that conversation, I believe. He said something about us both being here.'

'The reality is something quite different, unfortunately. He was...' Patrick checked over his paperwork. 'Out for a run is what he told them before I got there, which he absolutely shouldn't have done and I'm working on getting that struck out of any official business. But given that he'd already been cautioned...' He trailed off again.

'Why shouldn't he tell them that, sorry?'

Patrick looked at me over the lip of a sheet of paper. 'Aside from the fact that it makes a liar of him from that first interview, it's also not provable. He fed me some far-fetched story about snatching up the wrong phone and... it hardly matters now, really.'

I saw an opening. 'Snatching up the wrong phone?'

He shook his head. 'He said he picked up your phone by mistake.'

'But that would mean...' I paused and pulled my brow together as though I was trying to calculate a tax return without a sheet of scrap paper. 'But that would mean *my* alibi would disappear, if he told them that.'

Patrick lowered the sheet, then, and set his glasses on the table, too. 'Now, Agnes,' he spoke in a tone that I imagined he reserved for the rest of the wives he must deal with. 'Fin has told me about the problems you've been having recently and I can see how this may act as an irritant but truly, there's nothing in it. He wasn't trying to incriminate you for anything, he was only trying to...' He waved a hand around like that might conjure up an appropriate ending.

'What problems have I been having, Patrick?'

His eyes narrowed. 'Your...' He tapped the side of his head. 'Problems.'

Crazy? So Fin had laid a paper trail of his plans already, whatever they were. I wondered how much information Patrick might already have about the psychologist, too. Had Fin told him I was climbing the yellow wallpaper of our failed nursery, or had he fabricated other evidence against me for something? I didn't ask, or push.

'I see,' I answered, instead, then turned back to the task of coffee.

'Anyway, all of that and more aside, I think his best bet going forward is to try to rope in Irene, who I'm told you know about.'

Like a failed motor function, the coffee mug slipped through my grasp and knocked against the edge of the kitchen countertop. It bounced, turned and landed as a sprinkle of porcelain across the wood floor and I tried to leap out of the way of the shards. I didn't see Patrick move, but I soon felt his hand around my upper arm pulling me back from the moment with the sound of my name but muffled – underwater. I turned to face him and nearly expected bubbles to emerge from his mouth with each utterance.

'I said, are you okay, Agnes?'

'Yes, Patrick, sorry, I... I'm fine.' *Fucking outraged but fine.* I couldn't believe Fin had been so brazen about discussing her and that Patrick had been so quick to throw her name around in my own home. I felt the sudden urge to scrub the floors and bleach the sides and white sage the space clean of the male hypocrisy of it all. But instead I only said, 'Yes, I'm aware of the situation with Irene.'

'Sit down, would you?' Even when he was being caring, he still sounded curt. I followed instructions, though, took a seat at my own kitchen table and rested my head in my palm, like the tortured and downtrodden housewife I was being contoured as. 'For all his apparent chivalry, Fin is effectively trying to dodge admitting that he was with Irene at the time of Eliah's death and–'

'I'm sorry?'

He spoke slower. 'He was with Irene at the time of Eliah's death.'

'But he wasn't.'

He looked taken aback. His eyes fluttered and his head jerked. 'And you know that how, exactly?'

Because he was out for a run with my phone. I shook my head. 'I suppose I don't.'

'Right, there we are then.' He poured himself a coffee and, without offering me one, he came to join me at the table. Small acts of fuck-wittery really did make the modern man, I thought then, albeit not for the first time. I had to hope my shock at the horseshit situation was disguising any annoyance I might feel at

155

being parched in my own kitchen. 'My next pitstop after this is to visit Irene at the university to see how comfortable she is with my roping her into this. It's a rhetorical question, though, of course.' He sipped his drink and started to shove papers back into the case. 'The main thing is we'll be able to shake the witness and– Ah.' He snapped his fingers as though realising something. 'That'll be the part I haven't mentioned to you. How close are you to a... Janey, Jo, something-with-J...'

'Jessa. She lives over the road.'

'She's the eyewitness who can place Fin here at the time of the attack.'

'I'm not close to her,' I snapped without thinking.

'Good, because we'll be looking to shake that alibi once we get Irene on board.' He sipped his coffee and winced. 'Bitter. I like it.'

I laughed. 'You'll find plenty to be bitter about in this house.' I shared the sentiment without thinking but Patrick huffed in a way that suggested some amusement at least. 'I'm sorry, this is a difficult time, as I'm sure you can appreciate.'

'Not only that.' He leaned forward, then, and set a hand on my knee.

I tried to hold back from flinching, though it must have been the most intimate contact we'd ever had. 'But I'm led to believe things haven't exactly been tip-top between you and Fin for a little while now. Is that... I mean, I wouldn't want to speak out of turn.'

The change in him was breakneck in speed. I narrowed my eyes. 'Meaning?'

'Agnes, you're both having affairs.'

'Well I'm not anymore,' I snapped.

'Touché.' He broke our contact and sat back. 'Do you still love your husband?'

I raised an eyebrow. 'If you're about to proposition me...'

He held up both hands in a defensive gesture. 'Arsehole that I am, I like to think I'd pick a moment better than this one. Besides, it would be a conflict of interest.'

He was right; he was an arsehole. But the conflict-of-interest idea had only just occurred to me, and I slipped it into my back pocket like a Get Out of Jail for my future self. *Worst case scenario...*

'I love my husband,' I answered, then, 'but I don't like him much.'

'Yes, well.' He took another sip, only he didn't wince that time. 'I can see why that might be the case. We've been friends for years and I still don't find him a comfortable pill to wash down with whisky.' He stared hard at a spot on the table for a second or two, and I imagined him weighing the dos and don'ts for what to ask next. 'Do you think your husband has it in him to kill someone, Agnes? Because they'll ask you that, assuming they haven't already.'

I thought very carefully about my answer. 'Don't we all?'

'Even a perfect housewife such as yourself?'

Especially me. I smiled. 'Only when the toilet seat is left up too often.'

He huffed a laugh. 'Of course, every woman's gripe in life.' He stood, then, smoothed down his tie and reached for his briefcase. 'Thanks for your time, Agnes. Fin will be pleased to hear that you're on his side in all this at least. It never looks good for men when the wives start turning on them.' He laughed again, then, but it was a more sincere sound than before. 'Which will be why I don't have one, I suspect.'

He walked out of the kitchen and toward the front door without a further word, and I followed. It pained me how he moved about the space with so much familiarity.

'Patrick...' He turned when he heard me. 'How long will Fin be in custody?'

He tilted his head from side to side. 'I give it another day. There's the witness to consider now, but I'm led to believe it's early days with her, nothing concrete. They'll be searching the house soon.' He snapped his fingers. 'I forgot to mention that one, didn't I? I assume you've no objections.'

I shook my head: *I encourage them to.*

'You can't prove a murder because of motive alone, though, Agnes, so trust that he'll be fine. After all, he probably wasn't the only person with reason to kill the bloke.'

CHAPTER TWENTY-FOUR

I moved into Xara and Dermot's spare bedroom the day after Patrick visited. Jessa and Umi offered their spare room, too, but I thought living with the eyewitness was too on the nose, even by my standards. Besides, Jessa and Umi were blissful in their happiness. Meanwhile, from what I'd seen of their coupledom Xara and Dermot looked to love each other in peaks and troughs and that was the level of connection I felt most comfortable with. When I snatched a moment of quiet – in between Dermot carrying bags for me and Xara offering snacks, a meal, how about coffee? – I called Vi to tell her what I'd done.

'You could have come here.'

I smiled. 'And interfere with your man friend?'

'Please.' She huffed. 'I'm sleeping with him for you now.'

'Meaning?' I inched the curtain open and stared across to my dead home. 'You must be sleeping with him for a better reason than that. Fin can't even be speaking to him now that he's... in trouble.'

'Is that how you see Fin's situation; as a spot of trouble?'

'Violet, don't.'

There was a long pause. 'I don't know when Fin last called

about you. He obviously hasn't while he's been in trouble, as you so diplomatically put it. But when he's out, and when he finds out you've opted to live across the street from him for the foreseeable, do you not think his first course of action will be to discredit you by highlighting the fact that he's been speaking to a reputable psychologist on your behalf?'

'Your man is reputable?'

'Would I be having sex with someone who wasn't?'

I rolled the question around. 'Yes, yes I think you would.'

She laughed. 'You know what you're doing, I think. You seldom do anything unless you *know* what you're doing. But if at any point you need anything, including a room for the night that doesn't look as though it's been peeled and plastered from a Laura Ashley catalogue, you only need to call and I'll send a car.'

'Send a car?' I parroted. 'Are you high society courting a plebeian?'

'Agnes, darling...' Xara's voice crept up to me.

'I have to go. The lady of the house is calling.'

'Be mindful, Bertha, that attic wasn't built for a long-term stay,' Vi answered, then disconnected the call before I could compliment her referencing.

In answer to my endless wonder about how the wives filled their days, the immediate answer looked to be: by doing nothing. Unless Xara had cleared an otherwise hectic schedule so she could follow me from room to room asking whether I needed anything, which seemed like a waste of a Wednesday by anyone's standards. We were sitting in the living room together – her in an armchair, legs tucked beneath her; me on the sofa facing the window, so I could wistfully look outside whenever the dramatic in me fancied it – when a streak of colour quickly flitted through my eyeline: white, blue, bright yellow.

'I think a police car just went by.' I rushed to the window and moved to push away the old-fashioned netting.

'Agnes, don't...'

Balls to your netting, Xara.

'The views from upstairs are much easier.'

I had to swallow a laugh. Of course she would know the best views. She rushed ahead of me and darted into the front room which – following the layout of Eliah and Nicole's home – turned out to be hers and Dermot's bedroom. I looked for ties around the bedposts, lube bottles on the bedside; anything that might imply that they occasionally added chocolate chips or at the very least sprinkles.

Xara stood at the window looking down and I joined her. I hadn't had a phone call to let me know Fin would be released. But what other reason was there for another police car to be leaving tracks through our perfect village, if not to bring my darling back to me? The thought was fully formed and uncomfortably heavy as I watched the car swerve around the turning circle in a single movement. Though it failed my expectations when it slowed to a crawl and stopped, instead, outside of Eliah's front door. Seconds later the back passenger door opened and, looking every bit the perfect widow, Nicole appeared.

Xara actually gasped.

'Do you think she's in disguise?'

Nicole's hair, no longer a bright blonde, was instead a deep hazelnut. There were lighter streaks, visible only when she turned around to assess the other houses. Then she spoke to someone inside the car, shut the door and began the lonely walk up her path. She didn't have any bags, though, so I hoped the most logical assumption – that she was visiting to collect post and personal belongings – would turn out to be the correct one. Whoever was driving didn't wait for her to cross the threshold, and Nicole hardly waited for their emissions to leave the village's pristine atmosphere before she turned on her heel and headed straight towards–

'Stay up here,' Xara cautioned me in a tone that was too affirmative. It didn't suit her. Though I reasoned she likely didn't have cause to use it often.

There was a deep desire in me to smack her back into place but I knew the reaction wouldn't suit my new role. Instead, I glanced at her from hooded eyes, ones that I hoped looked tired with worry – after years of using expensive treatments to disguise such a thing. She squeezed my hand and left, patting the bed as she did as though giving me a further instruction to sit down. But I couldn't go that far. I followed her out and lingered out of sight at the top of the stairs, every bit the earwigging child ready for their parents to argue.

Xara shook herself and took a deep breath before she opened the door. 'Nicole–'

'Where is she?'

Who squealed? I wondered. Jessa and Umi were the only ones who knew I'd moved across here. *Unless Dermot is keeping his proverbial ties in someone else's bedside.*

Xara was in the middle of struggling through a lie when I started to tread the stairs behind her. Nicole watched me the entire way. Widowhood looked good on her. Her hair was different and even her style of clothes looked slightly chicer than it had before Eliah. Though that may have been city life rubbing itself around her, I thought, too, especially after so long in her Cath Kidston existence here. She kept her eyes fixed to me while the lie died on Xara's lips and, as I closed the gap further, even Xara fell back into her submissive role and stepped aside to clear the way for us both.

I sucked in what I hoped sounded like a shaky breath, to help the façade, then said, 'I'm so–'

I heard it before I felt it: skin on skin and the crack that comes with it. All the hands I've felt played out in a montage that had been poorly cropped: Mum when I was knee-high and she'd found– Cameron when I told him to go with– Fin, Fin, Fin– Eliah, once, when I'd begged for him to– The sting of it bit into my cheek, my head dropped and my hand flew to my face. I could taste the violence as the inside skin broke open and spilt the beginnings of blood into my mouth. My teeth must have clamped, I realised. I must have tensed for it.

'We should talk,' Nicole said, then she pushed past us both and walked through the open doorway to Xara's living room. She had the comfort and familiarity of someone who had spent a hundred couples' nights there.

Xara closed the door. 'I'll make coffee.' She pointed to my face. 'And I'll get some frozen peas for that.' I wondered whether a bruise was already unfolding. 'Go, sit.'

It struck me that Xara might not know whose side she was on now. But if I lost her as an ally would I lose the rest of the wives, too? I couldn't afford for that to happen. So I nodded my head in understanding and disappeared into the room. Nicole was sitting on the sofa where I'd been only half an hour earlier and I had the creeping sense of keeping this life warm for her. But when I landed in the armchair – as far away from her as I could manage – I realised the look she'd been giving me wasn't a cold one.

'That'll bruise,' she said.

I touched the skin lightly. 'It's not like I'm going out much.'

'No.' There was a long pause before she added, 'Fin will be out soon.'

'How do you... I mean, they told you that, the detectives?'

She nodded. 'You and he, you aren't on good terms?'

I huffed a laugh and winced at the discomfort of it. 'He doesn't know I've left.'

'And are you on good terms with anyone else's husband, or was it just mine?'

'Nicole, I...' I thought she likely expected another attempt at an apology but I couldn't muster one. I'd given her a free hit, after all. 'I was only sleeping with your husband, yes.'

She pulled in a shaky breath. 'I wasn't.'

It took longer than it should have. But when it clicked my eyes snapped wide and I couldn't stifle a smile. *Oh, to be a perfect housewife.* 'Is he anyone I know?' I asked, with a mixture of dread that I might be pushing my luck and excitement that she might say Dermot's name in a hushed tone. But instead she only shook her head and looked down at the carpet. 'That's why you left the event, on the day of Eliah...' I petered out as she started to nod. 'It's the person you told me about, all those weeks ago?'

She made a murmur of agreement. 'The others, they don't know.'

'Understood,' I answered plainly, and her head snapped up. It didn't feel like there was anything I needed to add, and from her faint smile I thought she felt the same. We were both silent, locked in that same knowing stare still, when Xara walked into the room carrying a tray with cups, saucers and a cafetière. When she set the tray on the table in the centre of the space, I couldn't help but notice that she'd opted against her favourite porcelain pattern; maybe she expected plates to be thrown.

'Is everything okay in here, ladies?'

Nicole cocked an eyebrow at me. 'It will be.'

'Bugger,' Xara said under her breath. 'I forgot the peas.'

CHAPTER TWENTY-FIVE

I 'd lost track of time, what with the excitement of my husband being detained on suspicion of murdering the man I was having an affair with and all. The dates and days had moved at a strange pace. It wasn't until Nicole had finally left – not just the house, but the village entirely, to head back to her sister's for as long as she needed – and I'd retreated to the bathroom to take advantage of Xara's free-standing tub that I saw the prompt I needed: an open packet of Bodyform.

'Fuck.'

I pressed the towels to my chest like a treasured artefact, which revealed the pale coloured boxes that had been hidden behind them. On one side, ovulation sticks; on the other, pregnancy tests.

'Fuck.'

The bath water ran so hot that it began to steam the room and I felt as though I'd fashioned a sauna from my panic. That, or the panic was bringing everything to a boil around me. Xara might miss a test, I thought, and there would be ample chance the next day to go out and buy my own. Yet, in my panic still, I found that I was tearing open the box and easing out a foiled packet. Not a minute later and I was sat on the toilet with my legs parted; the bath was near to full. In one of the many undignified positions women are expected to force themselves into, I slipped my hand – and the test – between my legs and willed the piss out of me. I felt myself clench around the stream, as though my body were somehow *that* desperate to avoid the result of something that it must already know. When the end of the test was soaked through, I rested it on the back of the toilet with a bed of paper beneath it, then wiped and put the lid down.

'How long can three minutes really take?' I whispered, then heard the stupidity of the question.

I snatched my phone from the shelf and thumbed in to set a timer. But the handset soon hummed alive in my palm with the arrival of a phone call. It was a withheld number and it felt far too late in the day for that to be the bringer of anything good. Still, it would perhaps be the distraction I needed. So I answered – 'Hello?' – with a cocksureness that bit me on the arse when the caller replied.

'I think you've got some explaining to do.'

'Fin.'

'Honey, I'm home.'

I looked at the locked bathroom door as though expecting him to knock against it. 'You're at the house.'

'Correct, and you are...'

'Staying with Xara and Dermot.'

'Because...'

I glanced over at the test: there was still no result. 'You're under suspicion of murder, Fin. Do you honestly think–'

He cut across me with a harsh laugh. 'You don't want to know what I honestly think, Agnes, at this point in time. Though I do think it would be sensible for you to pack up from your slumber party and make your way home, don't you? Think of how it looks, if nothing else.' Then he huffed. 'But I'd wager you know how it looks though, don't you? Which is exactly why you've done it.'

'I don't know what you mean.'

I thought of the ways in which this conversation might be recorded, and I resolved denial was the only means forward.

'Tell me, Agnes, how bored are you? In life, I mean. You're having an affair, you're toying with very dangerous breath play practices; because you told the police about that, didn't you? And now you're, what, framing me for... Is that it, Agnes, is that really what you're trying to do?'

'I'd have to be mad to try such a thing, though, wouldn't I, Fin?' I chanced another look: still nothing. The time on the call screen showed we'd been talking for nearly two minutes. 'Perhaps I am mad. Perhaps you should get me seen to.'

'So it's spite that's driven you to this, is it?'

It didn't matter how he framed the question; I was a big enough girl to know not admitting to anything would be my best friend here. Though I knew he'd get like a dog with a bone, too. I set a hand flat on my chest and felt the glitter of sweat there; I tapped against the damp skin to ground myself. But there was only so much benefit to be gained from counselling techniques when you were backed into a corner by a rabid animal. I didn't know whether he or I was the mutt here, though, and I didn't appreciate him making me feeling that way and– Knock.

A strangled sound died on my lips.

'Agnes, are you okay in there?'

Xara had knocked softly but I'd remembered the thump of his–

'Tell her you're fine,' Fin said quietly, as though she might somehow overhear him, and though I was resentful I found I was grateful for the instruction too.

'I'm sorry, Xara, everything is fine. I'm just having a soak.'

'You're talking to me in the bath?'

'Okay, darling. Shout one of us if you need anything.'

'Tell her you're fine.'

With Xara's words one side and Fin's the other I found they knocked together somewhere in my busy head and I tried to answer them both at once: 'Thank you.'

'Don't thank me, Agnes. I wanted rid of her to have you to myself.'

'Fin... I can't live with you while you're accused of murder.'

There came another huff. 'They've searched the house, did you know that?'

When? I wanted to ask but I couldn't give him the satisfaction of knowing something in this that I didn't. It might have happened while Nicole was busy confessing to her affair or Xara was busy plying us with cake that Nicole would have baked better; or while I was lying about how hideous, just positively hideous and shocking the situation with Finian was becoming. The police could have stripped the yellow wallpaper from my own home and there was a strong chance I would have missed it then. I was too desperate to keep in the fold with the wives to let anything be a distractor – including my husband.

In my silence, though, he let out a curt laugh. 'I hope you didn't have anything stashed away that shouldn't have been here.'

'Please, I've got nothing to hide.'

'Apart from being a murderer.'

The accusation kicked me in the ovaries. I looked at the test again, then, but didn't lean far enough forward to catch sight of the result. It wouldn't bring anything good: the panic of a pregnancy would ruin my game and the relief would be too observable to him, even through the phone line.

'That's a horrible thing to accuse your wife of.'

'But you don't mind accusing your husband of such a thing.'

'I haven't accused you of anything, Fin, I've only–'

'Left in the night like a Victorian whore fleeing a pimp.'

'Oh, please. It's late in our marriage for you to take such an interest in anything like my subject area or my work.'

'You have no work, Agnes, I took that from you. Remember?'

There was another painful turn in my stomach. *And I'll take everything you have...*

'Let's be frank with each other,' he spoke into my silence again. 'We deserve that at least, Agnes. You're sad that I've reduced you to a housewife. You had an affair. It happens. Though I don't think you're a murderer, I mean, the thought alone is ludicrous, but I do think you'll happily throw me under this bus as it goes speeding through our little village. How am I doing?'

I kept my voice neutral. 'No comment.'

'You might even know who the actual killer is, who knows? That isn't necessarily my business. Though if it's one of your local witches' circle then it would make a great headline, so don't rule out selling your story when you can. Am I warmer?'

'No comment.'

His tone changed to one of impatience then. 'For God's sake, Agnes, what's your endgame here? Will you see me pestered and probed for much longer? Work is breathing down my bloody neck. Not to mention I've put Irene in a terrible position as well. Although that was more Patrick's doing than mine but still. She's a patient woman but...'

And he really did talk for nearly a full thirty seconds about the inconvenience I was causing to his mistress. Until he circled back, as though remembering where his vitriol had started.

'When will this end, Agnes?'

I forced out a steady breath. 'I only want to see the proper person punished.'

'You spiteful bitch, Agnes, truly spiteful. Did you torture animals as a child?'

'Only once and I loved it.'

He fell so silent that I thought I could hear the tick of a clock in his background. I wondered which room of our home he might be having this conversation in. His face would be distorted now with the kind of confusion he wore when a grant proposal was turned down or the request for a sabbatical was rejected. There was a weight of smugness in my chest that I could still surprise him; it was important in a marriage.

I reached over the edge of the bath to check its temperature. 'My water's getting cold, Fin, was there anything else?'

'I hope it scalds you.'

'I love you too, sweetheart.'

I disconnected the call before he could throw another accusation or slur. He'd called me terrible things before and then typically took it back the morning after. He said once, in the same breath as an apology, that it was beneath him to use such base language. Yet, when the right buttons were pushed, it all came tumbling out. I'd wanted to ask more than once whether it was mother or father tongue that had taught him how to speak that way, but the opportunity had never come up.

With my phone in hand still, I took two greedy in- and exhales to steady myself before I leaned forward and grabbed the ten-minute old test from the back of the toilet. I hadn't thought to check whether there was a time limit on the result. But I decided to take another one, just to be sure.

CHAPTER TWENTY-SIX

Xara and Umi felt like they talked me into it; which is exactly what I wanted for them. Jessa – and the unfortunate Dermot, who had been dragged kicking and screaming into the conversation – thought I should do what felt right. But she undercut the comment with a follow-up about how an early dinner with a friend never hurt anyone.

I'd already told Vi that dinner and drinks would be a perfect remedy for the shit-mess around me. When the wives had given me their approval for a night away from their nest, though, I slipped away on the pretence of calling Vi to confirm. They all thought my arm was twisted: mangled with persuasion. Umi even kept me company while I got ready. At the vanity table in the room that looked more and more like my space rather than Xara's, I painted on a thin edge of lip liner around bright red lips. Fin always hated this shade on me. Umi watched me in the mirror, and when I puckered she cocked an eyebrow and smirked.

'You look like a woman ready to take names and numbers.'

I snorted. 'I don't need their names.'

'Agnes.' She leaned forward and softly tapped the back of my arm. 'Are you–'

'I'll stop you right there, Umi, I am nothing.'

She closed the gap between us, then, and set a hand on either of my shoulders. We locked eyes in the mirror as she started to knead my skin. 'Don't ever say that about yourself. Okay?' She waited for me to nod. 'If you wanted some fun tonight then no one could blame you.'

'Agnes!' Jessa shouted from downstairs. 'There's a car for you.'

I stood up, then, and Umi linked arms with me as I headed for the door. 'Besides which, whoever this Violet is, I very much like her style.'

I laughed. 'I'll let her know...'

Violet was waiting in the outside foyer of the restaurant for me with a smile and a lit cigarette. 'Can I tempt you?'

'Is this a trap?' I leaned forward to kiss her cheek.

'Please, I'm not your husband.' But still, I shook my head at the offering. 'Suit yourself.' When she'd dubbed out the cigarette she pulled a small bottle of perfume from her bag and spritzed one side then the other. Next, she pulled out breath mints.

'What else do you have in there?'

'A magician never reveals her tricks. Ready?' She held out her arm and I accepted. 'I've heard good things about this spot but I've never been here. We can lose our virginities to the place together.' She changed her tone to speak to the front of house who was waiting at a podium inside. 'Table for–'

'Violet,' he finished for her. Vi threw him a quizzical look and he laughed. 'You don't remember me.'

She looked him up and down, then, and tilted her head to one side then the other. 'No, I'm not sure I do. I have a table booked.'

His smiled faded to an expression of understanding. 'This way.'

'Is there anyone you haven't slept with in this city?' I whispered from behind her.

'God, I hope so.'

'Will this table suit?' he asked as he turned.

It was a beautiful spot next to a stained-glass window. Between that and the rain, the city looked doused in watercolour. The room was dimly lit with industrial lighting, exposed but low-watt bulbs hanging everywhere. It was mostly tables for two inside the dining area, with chairs that were so high-backed they afforded the diners a good measure of privacy, and I wondered what that said of their expected clientele. It struck me that we'd spend our evening surrounded by businessmen and their mistresses – which perhaps spoke volumes about me and Vi.

'This is perfect, Alex,' she answered, and the man smiled as though someone had just pulled his six numbers, such was the power of being recognised by Vi. She reached and took his hand. 'Thank you.'

Alex – now that he'd been christened – pulled out Vi's seat then mine. He promised our menus would be with us shortly and disappeared wordlessly back to his desk duty, clutching whatever Vi had passed over during their contact.

'Violet, did you tip that man?'

She nodded. 'Yes, with a business card that has a dead number on it. Now can we talk about your problems?'

'I don't have problems. I'm not the one accused of murder.' A young waiter came to a stop at our table with two menus at that moment. And his face looked as though he'd

173

been slapped with one or both of them. 'You're a love, thanks.' I reached and took the slim binders. 'We'll have a bottle of your house red.'

'Agnes...' Vi waited until I turned to her. 'You're drinking?'

But I only looked back at the waiter. 'House red, two glasses, please?'

'Of course.'

'As I said,' I restarted when we were alone, 'I'm not accused of murder. I have little to nothing to worry about. Fin, on the other hand–'

'Is here.'

'What?'

I craned around the side of my chair and there he was: my darling husband. Irene looked different to when I'd last seen her, though, and she'd obviously dressed up for the occasion too. Fin was wearing a crisp white shirt with a navy-blue trim around the fold of his collar, paired with navy trousers and a blazer hung over his arm. She wore her hair in curls that made her look like a character from a children's narrative, and I wondered whether that's what he liked in her: there was nothing he'd need to change. Her skirt was an acceptable length: not so long that she looked prudish; short enough that he could fuck her in the bathroom if the urge took him. She was wearing a floral blouse – cream with flowers in a polka dot – and a red poncho draped around her shoulders. It compounded the fairy-tale look of her. Even more so given that she was out with a wolf.

Fin pulled her close to him as they walked through the space; a hand around her waist so tight that it would have made it hard for her to walk. Irene was making pleasant talk with the waiter while Fin scanned the room and–

I jumped back into the safe cubicle of my seat. 'Did he see me?'

'Arsehole,' Vi answered under her breath. 'Yes, he saw you. Don't get comfortable, Agnes, we're leaving.'

'Is he coming over?'

'No, he's blissfully ignoring you so he can spend an evening with her.' She reached under the table for her bag. 'Put your coat back on.'

I set a hand flat on my stomach and forced a breath out. 'I need the bathroom.'

'Fine,' she huffed in a tone that I thought she likely reserved for her men. 'I'll get the bottle to go and I'll meet you in the foyer. Do you need anything?' She was already standing, though, and shifting away from the table small steps at a time. I only shook my head, stood and moved in the opposite direction, heading for the neon sign in the far corner of the room.

The toilets were lit by the same unforgiving glare that lit these spaces the land over. There was no one else there. I leaned against the edge of an empty sink and breathed in and out slowly, to steady whatever was racing through me. I'd cracked myself into so many parts: wife; friend; bitch; murderess; fraudster; witness. When I had panicked reactions to anything then, I no longer knew which bit of me the panic belonged to. I hit the cold tap and held my hands under it. My make-up had taken too much effort to ruin so I wouldn't wash my face. But I splashed my wrists, held them under the stream and focused on the reflection of my stomach; there was a new sense of this place as my core.

When the door behind me swung open I didn't think to look up. But there's a creeping recognition that comes over anyone when someone stands behind them for too long. I glanced up to check myself in the mirror and there he was, my darling husband again.

If I hadn't known better I would have said it was superhuman, the speed at which he moved from one position to another. He threw me hard against the nearest wall and wrapped a hand tight around my throat and– Knock. I tried to blink away all the flashbacks. He held me a little too high, so I was forced onto my toes, and I struggled to keep my balance even with him against me. When he squeezed gently and applied pressure, I– Knock. I blinked away the beginnings of watering eyes and tried to force a swallow which only added to the feeling of his force. He leaned a little harder against me and– Knock.

'You think safe gestures still work here?' he asked, his teeth so tight with anger that the words struggled to pass. 'I'll listen to your safe gestures when you tell me what mine is, Agnes. How's that for a deal? What's *my* safe word?'

He pulled away so suddenly that I lost my balance. My knees threatened to give out beneath me and my hands rushed to my throat in immediate defence.

'You're out for a meal with your mistress,' I struggled to throw. 'You're out with her and asking for favours from me.'

Fin moved closer, then, so spittle landed on my ear as he spoke. 'She's a placeholder, sweetheart. When you've finished your little housewife's revolt, she goes. For now, she's my alibi in this little game of yours, so don't judge me too harshly for treating her well.' He kissed my cheek softly and then stepped back to a safer distance. There was a good metre between us, and I felt my breathing ease. 'Give Violet my best.'

When the door banged closed behind him, I let my knees bend as I slid down the wall and landed in a crouch. There was a swell of feeling in my belly so knotted that I couldn't pull arousal apart from malice. I was midway through counting my breathing – my fingers plucking at the knit in my gut – when I felt the hum of my mobile in my clutch. *She's worried.* I imagined Vi standing in the foyer with a cigarette in one hand

and her phone in the other. But when I freed the handset it was a different name: Xara.

'Agnes, I'm so sorry to call.' She didn't wait for a hello and while I pressed here and there at the tender skin forming around my throat, I didn't mind. 'The lights have been off in your house all evening, but about half an hour ago we saw a chap go inside. God, we sound like such nosy–'

'Don't worry what we sound like,' Umi snapped in the background.

'Look, he must have had a key, because since he went in the lights have snapped on and there's a normal amount of life in the place and– Well, he hasn't come rushing out with your treasured belongings but– I'm sorry, Agnes, we were worried.'

I forced a swallow. *Would Patrick pay a house call without Fin being there – and with his own key?* But I couldn't think of any other suspects.

'What did he look like, Xara?'

'Six foot, I'd say. Dark brown hair, glasses. White button-down shirt with short sleeves; Umi thought she saw a tattoo, a sleeve thing. He was wearing tailored trousers, though, the kind you might wear to work, and there was an overnight bag and... I can't say more for how he looked, Agnes, I'm sorry. Umi is about ready to go over there and knock on the door, if that will set your mind at ease?'

I smiled at their comradery. When I ran my hand through my hair I felt the damp of sweat in my roots, even with the cool comfort of the tiled wall behind me. 'It's okay, Xara, you can call off the dogs. I know who it is.'

'Oh, thank God, because let me tell you...'

Cameron. Fin has found Cameron.

BEFORE

Violet passed the joint back to me. I exhaled hard and spluttered a laugh on my out-breath. Vi laughed, too, although we were both well past the point of knowing what was funny. My flatmates were out for the evening. And after a particularly gruelling week of post-graduate study, wherein our lecturers – in the English and Psychology departments respectively – had ploughed us hard with their expectations of our cohorts for the coming semester, the only thing either of us felt fit to do was absolutely nothing. I heard the joint crackle as Vi pulled in again, then she set it on the ashtray in the windowsill and crossed the room to an abandoned beanbag. Another laugh tumbled out of her as she landed in the centre of it.

'I'm never getting out of this.'

I breathed out like a dragon and I felt powerful in it. 'You'll have to pay rent.'

'Invoice me.' She waved the idea away, like my threat was nothing. Though for her I suppose it wasn't. The rent for her own place – a place she didn't share with anyone – came directly out of her father's bank account at the end of every month. She'd once told me that money was nothing; for people like her I guessed it wasn't. She laughed again, then, and said, 'So what's happening with the TA?'

I sucked in hard to keep my mouth busy. I couldn't stifle the smile though. 'Nothing,' I said as the smoke escaped. 'He isn't teaching many of my classes this semester, so I'll hardly even see him.'

She snorted. 'He'll make sure you see him.'

'Why do you think that?'

'A man like him?' She managed to lift her head to get a look at me but I could tell the movement was an effort. 'They don't let a woman go until they've got them. He'll be an easy catch for you, Ag, if you're into it.'

'I don't think I want easy.'

She smirked. 'No... You like the chase, don't you?'

'Oh, please.' I rolled my eyes. 'Don't bring your psych class in here.'

'Psych class has nothing to do with it.' Vi pushed and shoved on the outside of the beanbag, then, and huffed and struggled until she was upright. The only times I'd ever seen her inelegant were in these moments, when we were baked beyond reason. And the laughter erupted out of me again. 'You can fuck off.' She pointed behind her. 'Do you know how hard that thing is to get out of?'

I cocked an eyebrow. 'Imagine how hard it is to have sex in it.'

'Oh, Agnes.' She started to brush the back of her jeans down in a hurry. 'You haven't?'

'Once.'

'Well, I imagine once was enough. Give me.' She held a hand out and I obliged. 'Don't you think you might like something easy, love? A little rough and tumble with a stuffy academic type.' With her free hand she reached up to push a stray hair back behind my ear.

'I'd hardly call him stuffy.'

I looked out of the window, then, and down to the path that ran between my block of flats and the next. There was a young couple there, only identifiable from the closeness of their silhouettes, and I thought of how Cameron had pressed himself against me during the Christmas party before we'd all scarpered home for the holidays. Vi had caught us in a hallway, his one knee pressed into the space between my own, and he'd pushed away from me like an electrical current had coursed through him as soon as he heard her voice. It had taken the rest of the evening for me to forgive her for the interruption.

'What about Michael?'

I grimaced. 'From linguistics?'

'I imagine he's good with his tongue. Think of all those rolling sounds in the Eastern languages.'

I belched out another laugh. 'You're terrible.'

'You're thinking of him.'

'I'm not thinking of Michael.'

'You know that's not who I meant.'

There was something about Cameron that had slipped under my skin. He was teaching modules that I hadn't elected to take for the second semester, though, and there was no moving around that. I looked back out of the window and sighed when I spotted the couple had gone.

'There's a departmental mixer happening in week four,' she announced, and my head snapped around. 'I'm on good terms with my course lead.'

'I'll bet you are.'

The joint was burning down to its end and I reached to take it from her. Instead, Vi snatched it further away and craned to take another deep inhale herself. When her mouth was full, she set the index finger of her free hand under my chin and pulled me towards her. I opened my mouth a fraction as she rounded her lips into an O, and then smoke tumbled out from her in a slow exhale. I drew the breath in, held it for a second, then tipped my head back before I let the air out.

'Tell me about the mixer,' I asked.

She dubbed the joint out and dusted her hands off. 'Humanities, social sciences, all the rest of the elbow-patches, they're getting together to drink and share the war stories of academia. Apparently there'll be some announcement through the portal closer to the time. It'll be made open to all PG students, in the interest of getting us all to...' She made a waving motion with her fingers. 'I don't know, mingle or something. Christ knows what they think we've been doing for the last five months already.'

I smiled. 'Some have mingled more than others.' I nudged her ankle with my foot. 'Be my date for the evening?'

'I'll be your date there, but I'm not being your date home.'

'Deal. Drink?'

She nodded, so I stood and trod towards the kitchen. It was one of those blissful moments of not realising how out of it you are until you try to use your basic faculties. I felt my way along the wall to make sure I didn't collapse on route. Then I pulled chilled wine from the fridge and searched for clean glasses while Vi steadied herself in the doorway. In the corner of my eye I could see her looking around the compact space and I knew what she was thinking.

'The offer stands, you know,' she said as I handed her a drink. 'If you wanted to–'

'We'd kill each other if we lived together.'

'Agnes, don't be dramatic, of course we wouldn't. You wouldn't even have to–'

'Pay rent, you've mentioned, Vi. But I happen to like paying rent.' I took my drink and shuffled past her. 'I'm making good money on the essays, though, and I can afford this place easily enough. I'll have money saved for my own place too, by the time my funding application is complete for the doctorate.' I'd spent the last five months making ends meet by writing undergraduate essays; tailored to the needs of each idiot with funds enough to pay people like me. 'It makes me feel like an evil genius,' I said, my tone jovial. On my way back in I dodged the beanbag that lay battered in the centre of the room and instead dropped onto the sofa. Vi took the opposite end.

'Feet,' she instructed, and I swung my legs up. She kneaded at the soles of my feet like they were hours away from forming good bread. 'Be careful, Agnes. I worry what will happen to that bright future of yours if you get caught–'

'I won't get caught out, Vi.'

He didn't have his own office. But as a teaching associate with an office hour, he was afforded the office space of Dr Buddy – arsehole in nature, despite the name – to run appointments with students three times a week. He emailed me to ask me to attend his Wednesday session and with a stomach flip that embarrassed me I replied to ask whether there was a good time.

'At your convenience. Best. C.'

I didn't tell Violet.

Cameron called me in when I peered around the door of the office, even though he was on the phone to someone when I got there.

I shuffled in and took a seat wordlessly, then folded my hands in my lap while I waited. It was impossible not to eavesdrop at such a close range – 'I don't know that that's quite right for the module...' – but I tried to distract myself with a good glance around the room – 'I've got free time to talk this through in person, if...' – and, when I thought I could get away with it, I stole looks at him. He wore a dark green shirt and a waistcoat, glasses that rested on the end of his nose in a way that made me wonder whether he needed them. He was every bit the cliché and when I saw him in that light I wondered what the attraction was. But of course, the attraction was as much about the throb I felt when he dissected literary frameworks with a flaming fierce enough for the bedroom as it was about anything else.

'I've got a student here at the minute and...' he said, and my concentration snapped with the sting of a rubber band. 'I'll see you next week... Excellent, thanks ever so much... Bye now.' He ended the call and threw the phone on the desk.

'That sounded like a hard effort,' I said, my tone light.

He only grunted, though, and pushed a hand through his mess of hair. Without saying anything further, he snatched at his bag from beneath the desk, hauled it up and ripped out a wad of paper. It landed with a thud between us.

He knows.

'It's not your best work.' He leaned back in the chair opposite me and fixed me with a stare that felt more sexual than it did accusatory. But that likely said more about me than it did him. It was hard to disentangle panic from being caught with the hot relief at being in a room with the man.

I leaned forward to check the title of the essay. 'She's a 2:2 student,' I said as I dropped back. 'Anything higher and–'

'It would have looked suspicious.' He laughed, then, and relaxed his expression. 'You're very clever, Agnes.'

The compliment tugged at my insides. 'Not clever enough.' I nodded at the paper. 'What was my tell?'

'I'm not likely to tell you that, otherwise you'll know what to avoid next time.'

'There won't be a next time,' I answered at such a speed that it sounded rehearsed – which it was, of course. Vi had been waiting for this capture since the essay scam had started but I'd been cocksure in my belief she was wrong. That didn't mean I hadn't prepared, though. 'Look, the other PG students have a different life to me. They have people looking out for them... people who care. I...' I tried to sound as tortured as I could about it all. 'I'm different.'

'I know.'

I chanced a look at him, then.

'They'll kick me out for this.'

'I know that, too.'

'So...' I let the unsaid question hang there for a second before I shrugged. 'Should I pack up my room?'

'Pack up your business. I want you to actually stop doing this.' He tapped the coversheet of the assignment. 'You've got a bright future, Agnes, and you shouldn't be pissing that away on half-cocked essays for silver spoon students in their first year. If they don't have brains big enough to make the most of their opportunities here then they surely don't deserve the likes of your skills in helping them.' I wasn't sure what face I made but whatever it was he laughed again, then added, 'Apologies for being frank. But while we're on it...' He stood and crossed around to the other side of the desk, close by to me, then he perched on the edge. I didn't like being spoken down to but I thought I should let him have it. 'I know that what I say about you doing this or not doing it isn't going to make a damn difference to whether you actually do it or not.'

I opened my mouth in immediate protest but he held a finger up.

'Don't. I like to think you respect me too much to tell another lie.'

So I only nodded, and relaxed back into the chair.

'But the deal I'm going to make you is this: if you get caught, I knew nothing.'

I didn't need to think on it. But I bunched my mouth up at one side and took a slow glance around the room. The space was everything I wanted for myself, and I knew an academic offence like essay writing would land it further away. Though lack of funding for my studies wasn't going to help the situation either. I stood, then, pulled my skirt back down to an acceptable length, and held out a hand.

'You've got yourself a deal.'

He reciprocated the gesture. 'Thanks for dropping in, Agnes.'

'Thanks for having me.' I smiled and then turned to leave. I was halfway out the door when he spoke again.

'You'll be at the departmental mixer in a couple of weeks.'

It didn't feel like a question.

Forgiveness was step nine. Dad had made the phone call for her, though, which didn't bode well for the success of the weekend in total. Still, I dropped my bag in the hallway – 'Pop, I'm home.' – slapped on a smile the likes of which I typically reserved for potential employers and men I was trying to get into bed, and I trod the length of the hallway to where I could hear them both rattling around the kitchen. There were hushed tones, too, until I was only a few steps away at which point they stopped; it was like a flashback to my childhood. Only now we all had to pretend that the disdain we felt towards my mother's alcoholism had withered away somehow, now I was old enough to understand it as a sickness; though the resentment was still fierce, and steadfastly carried into adulthood. I wore my hatred of her behaviour in the same way Dad wore the scars of it; open and ugly, hardly concealable. He was clearly able to overlook it, though, if he was here giving her another chance – or rather, another-another chance.

I smiled when I saw her shrunken figure in the corner of the kitchen. Then I told the first lie of the afternoon. 'You're looking well, Mum.'

Dad crossed the room, grabbed me by the elbow and kissed my cheek. 'It's so nice to have you home, Aggie.' He was the only person who ever called me by that pet-name; that is to say, he was the only person I'd allow to use it. He steered me towards the table – already laid for dinner – and pulled out a chair. 'We've done a full roast. Your mother's been at it all day and I've felt like a right spare through it all. You haven't let me do a thing, have you? Do you want a drink, Aggie? Red wine still?' The questions rushed out of him like vomit might and he soon realised his mistake. 'Oh. Oh, I–'

'I've got some non-alcoholic, in the...' Mum petered out when she saw me stare across at her, but she pointed to the fridge.

'Wine, Aggie?' Dad already had a hand on the fridge. 'Squash?'

There isn't a drink in the world more at-home-with-the-parents than squash. 'Blackcurrant, please.'

But when he yanked the door open a small, 'Oh,' fell out of Mum. He closed the door and looked her way. 'I only got orange. I... I forgot and I only got...'

'That's okay.' Dad reached around to rub at her arm. 'It's okay, love. Agnes?'

'Fake wine or water is fine, whatever you've got chilled.' Orange squash tasted like childhood sickness and sore throats. I'd hated it since I hit my teens. 'Do you need any help with dinner or... I don't know, anything I can be doing?'

Mum smiled. 'Sit there and be waited on.'

'Great.' I stared down at my empty hands on the table. 'Don't let me get idle.'

They kept my mouth busy at least with chat about my end of year dissertation plans – that they had no understanding or appreciation of – and talk of Violet, who they'd been enamoured with since first meeting her. They didn't remember the names of my housemates, though, so Dad only asked a general, 'And how's everyone else?'

Only minutes after that, Mum was lumping butter in with boiled potatoes when she questioned me about any love interests, in a tone that made me think she didn't expect an answer. Faced off with that question, I found that I thought of Cameron like a knee-jerk and I didn't care for it. So instead of mentioning the names of men who I'd slept with once or twice and discarded – of which it suddenly felt like there were plenty to choose from – I only shrugged and changed the subject to PhD funding: something else they wouldn't understand, and therefore wouldn't probe too hard at. We could have been strangers getting to know each other for the ways in which we carefully trod around the details of our lives, somehow without really revealing anything at all.

'It's like you've settled right in, if you're thinking of staying up that way,' Dad said, and he set the last of many dishes on the table. He kissed the crown of my head before crossing round to his own side and taking a seat. 'We're proud of you, Aggie. Aren't we, Shawna? Dead proud of her.'

Mum was sitting by then, too, and she reached across to take Dad's hand when he offered it. The sight of their domestic bliss sent a roll of something through my stomach that I tried to laugh off as hunger. He'd obviously forgiven her for the boiling water to the face; the flung hairdryers; and the broken plates. I assumed that my forgiveness was next in line – at least, they expected it to be.

I tugged at the sleeve of my cardigan to pull the fabric over the thick scar that ran from my left thumb up to my wrist. 'Well, this looks great. You shouldn't have gone to so much fuss, though, it's only me.' I smiled at Dad and threw a glance Mum's way. She looked nervous. *Good*, I thought before turning my attention to the food. 'I don't know that I'll stay for the whole weekend, if I'm honest, I've got a boatload of work to do back at home that needs–'

Mum interrupted me with a laugh. 'Isn't this home?'

I met her stare. 'No.'

'Agnes...' Dad warned but I only raised an eyebrow at him and carried on with my serving of green beans.

'Like I said, there's a lot of work waiting for me back at home.'

'We've been doing a lot of work here, haven't we, Tim?' Mum tried to lighten her tone. 'Agnes, I know we haven't talked much about it, but a lot... there's been a lot...' False starts stuttered out of her. She tried and failed three times to kickstart the sentiment before sighing and lowering her head. 'I'm trying to say that I've been doing a lot of work, on myself, on the recovery programme and... I'm doing well.'

I waited in case there was more coming. Dad threw me a pleading look, so I glanced back to Mum and smiled. 'That's great. Could you pass the bread?'

Dad sighed but followed instruction. 'Home-made, that is.'

'Very impressive.'

'Your mother got up at the crack of dawn to get it just right.'

I took a roll and set it down on the small plate next to my dinner one, then I passed the rest back across the table. 'Why don't you just ask me and get it over with?' I was busy serving portions of vegetables onto my plate so I didn't see it, but in their quiet I imagined a look passed between them. 'Forgiveness, right?' I looked up, then, and saw Mum's eyes fill with tears as though I'd ripped adhesive away from an infected wound. She pursed her lips and slowly nodded. 'So ask.'

'Agnes, you're not making this a safe space for you mother to–'

'I'm sorry?' I belched out. I couldn't contain the outrage. '*I'm* not making this a safe space? While I'm sitting across from the woman who drunkenly threw a kettle of water over my father, while I watched. *I'm* the one making this a hostile environment.'

'Tim, she doesn't have to forgive me anything, you know–'

I kicked back from the table and thumped the surface of it with my fists. 'Don't defend me.' Rage bubbled up like a demon thing and I realised then that I was shaking with it. Mum and I stared each other down and in my peripheral vision I saw Dad glance between the two of us; an innocent bystander, like he'd always been in matters of us women. 'I don't forgive you and she's right,' I turned to face Dad, 'I don't have to. So if that's the reason you invited me back, and we've hastily managed to get it covered, then I may as well grab my bag from the hall and head home.'

Neither of them said anything. But they both watched me leave.

———

The departmental mixer was a mess of lecturers, students and the teaching associates that existed in the beautiful in between. It was largely an elbow-rubbing exercise for the middle-class white males, of which there were many.

I saw Cameron only once – head thrown back, mouth agape mid-laugh at something hilarious that a woman more beautiful than me had just said to him – and I decided in that drunken moment to draw a line under whatever sights I'd set on him.

There were enough of his kind to sample without muddying the waters by choosing someone who had a secret over me already. So I scanned the room for another body that might do. Even Vi had critiqued my behaviours with men since the visit to my parents weeks before. But she was too busy distracting her course leader that night to notice when I strayed from her, first into the huddle of linguistics students and later into the vague open water of philosophy.

No one else from my own course seemed to have turned up. Likely a good thing, given that Vi had taught me not to shit where you eat. Though things were complicated in that vein when it came to a teaching associate for–

'Agnes, are you lost?'

I was mid-conversation with someone too stupid for me to take home when I heard Cameron's voice behind me. I felt his fingertips lightly touch my elbow to pull my attention around. It was the first contact we'd had.

'Dr Buddy was looking for you,' he lied. I don't know how I knew it. But something in his tone wasn't altogether sincere. 'I'm not sure where he is now.' He looked over my head to scan the room. 'Sorry, chaps, may I cut in? Wouldn't want to keep a lecturer waiting and all.'

The other men laughed along; the one other woman in the huddle laughed a little too hard, and I wondered whether she was glad to get their attentions back. Cameron's grip tightened around my elbow as I said my goodbyes. We were out of earshot when he spoke again, but still he moved closer and dropped words right into me.

'I thought I'd never get you out of there.'

I laughed. 'I didn't need rescuing.'

'Your face said otherwise. This way.' He pushed a door open at the back of the room and waited for me to step ahead of him.

'Are we going to Dr Buddy's office?' I tried to swallow the smile forming.

'Don't be ridiculous, Agnes.' He caught up with me, set a hand on each shoulder and pulled me back until my spine curved against his stomach. 'He never comes to these things; he can't bloody stand them.'

I span around then stepped away to put a decent gap between us. 'I haven't written any more essays that need grading, if that's what you're collaring me for.'

He cocked an eyebrow. 'I didn't realise I'd thrown a leash around your neck.' He leaned against the wall, then, and pulled an e-cigarette from his inside pocket. 'Do you mind if I...' he petered out when I shook my head. 'The old boys in there are enough to drive anyone to addictive behaviours, don't you think?'

I tried very hard not to think of my mother. 'Mind if I...' He handed it over and I pulled in a hungry drag. Smoke billowed out of me as I answered, 'The old boys in there are looking for an excuse to dick measure, dress up their PG students in pretty clothing, and compare grade averages. Don't you think?' I landed on the wall next to him and pulled in another breath of smoke. 'Forgive me for being frank.'

'I like frank on you.'

How frank to be though, I wondered as I exhaled, inhaled, exhaled and used the time smoking to fill the space where my answer should have been. 'Okay, well at the risk of being frank again for the second time in as many minutes, I'm not sure why you felt the need to save me from the theories of life.'

He laughed. 'I thought it was about time we talked more, that's all.'

'Talked about?'

He shrugged. 'Games.' When I didn't answer he added, 'The ones we've been playing, the ones we could...' He pushed himself away from the wall, then, and stood closer to me. He rested a hand either side of my arms, his palms flat. 'I have a feeling I can trust you with something, Agnes. Am I right in thinking that?'

I tilted my head and made a show of thinking. 'Murder? Probably not. Sexual preferences? Probably.'

He laughed again and my pelvis dipped at the sound. 'Do you have a safe word?'

Violet was talking to me but everything was underwater: her voice and my vision of her blurred to the point of indiscernible. My whole body shook with such a force that I worried I might wear through her sofa, but the more I tried to control it the less I could steady myself. The quiver hadn't stopped since I'd stumbled out of Cameron's living room, hallway, front door and I'd tumbled through the city campus to find my way back to Vi. But nothing could still me. I felt the pinch of her cupped palms around the balls of my shoulders as she dropped to her knees to fall in my sight line. I'd been fixated on a spot on her floor for more seconds than I'd been able to count. The numbers had swum in and out of sequence and I thought it had likely been either a full minute or as many as thirty.

'Agnes!' Her voice broke through whatever was around me, then, and I flinched at the intrusion. 'Agnes, love, I need you to stay with me, okay?' She clicked her fingers; sharp bursts of noise that set me twitching but at least it had dulled the shakes. 'Stay with me, love, okay? I'm here and you can stay with me.' Her hands moved from my arms to my face to hold my stare in place on her. 'I need you to tell me what you did, love, okay? I need for you to tell me that.'

I nodded like I understood the request, but I couldn't form words still.

'Agnes, tell me what you did.'

'He asked for me to hurt him,' I managed.

Vi frowned and shook her head. 'I don't understand, love, what do you...'

'He asked for me to hurt him and I did.'

She nodded, then, and brushed matted hair away from my forehead. I hadn't realised I was sweating. 'Okay, love. Stay with me, Agnes, you're doing so well.' She kissed my forehead and I wondered what my brow must taste like. 'He asked for you to hurt him, and you did. And then what?'

The shaking that had only just started to still came in waves, then great lurches like I might bring up the ocean of water Vi had fed me since I arrived. I swallowed hard to still the rise of it all and tried to force a stream of air through rounded lips.

'And I didn't stop.'

CHAPTER TWENTY-SEVEN

The office was quiet enough for me to hear Annie Lennox playing in the waiting room. Like a nervous tic, I found my foot was tapping along in a movement that felt involuntary, though I wondered whether it was about the only thing helping me stay fixed to the seat. The room was a different one to where we usually met, and the change in location – added to the outright stress of the mess I'd found myself in – had catapulted me into something near to blind panic: small feet kicking at my innards, coupled with soft and sweeping motions as the anxiety turned over in me. *What fucking chaos...* The track outside changed – another Lennox song, one I didn't recognise – and my foot lost rhythm, and just like that I was up and pacing the room. There were certificates boasting a name I didn't recognise either; though the man had clearly done well for himself. I ran a hand through my hair and gripped at the back of my head as I circled the desk. There, pride of place, was a family portrait featuring that very man with all the certificates, and his beautiful wife, and their three nuclear children. I wondered how long it had taken them to conceive: *Were you little ones planned?* I bent to get a closer look at their smiles just as the door opened.

'I'm so sorry to keep you waiting, Agnes.'

I shot upright and hurried back to the side of the desk I belonged on. 'It's okay, really, I appreciate all of this has been short notice.'

He looked around. 'No Finian?'

I flashed a tight smile and dropped into the visitor chair. 'No, just me.'

Dr Neilson was holding a file, which he quickly snapped closed as though shutting me out of my own body. But he'd have to tell me what was in there sooner or later. I smiled again, softer, when he sat down opposite me. Rather than opening the file, though, he set it to one side and clasped his hands in front of him.

'There's a problem with the ultrasound in my office and I think our best route forward for today will be to scan you.'

'You've found something.'

He laughed. 'It isn't quite a growth, Agnes.' When I didn't reciprocate his humour his smile died on his lips and he took on a sterner tone. 'Why don't we get you stripped down and we'll take a look at what's happening?'

'That's the best offer I've had all day,' I answered, to try to inject some of our usual rapport. I reminded myself that I was likely only minutes away from asking the man for a favour. 'Don't bother pulling the curtain, doc, it's nothing you haven't seen before,' I added, as I crossed into the adjoining examination room. The walls were an offensive peach colour. *Probably something subliminal in that.* The chair and the stirrups were the same old that you'd find anywhere, though. I was midway through pulling my tights down when the doctor stopped me.

'I thought there'd been a spot of confusion there.' He even

set a hand on my arm and I wondered whether he was allowed to do that. 'I need your stomach, not your unmentionables.'

I laughed. 'To some those two things are one and the same.'

'Not in this office. Hop up.' He gestured to the seat. 'If you could pull the waistband of your skirt down and your top... atta girl.' I was already following instructions. 'Here Comes The Rain Again' was playing in the waiting room now and I found I was humming along. 'Dolores out front will be delighted to know there's another Lennox fan in the building. It's all I've all heard all bloody day,' he narrated as he went about setting up the machine. 'This will be the tiniest bit...' I winced as the gel made contact with the soft of my belly. 'Cold.'

'No trouble.'

I decided then that the next time I had a vaginal examination, instead of counting the ceiling tiles, I would count the amount of times I, woman, must have told doctor, man, that it didn't matter if he made me uncomfortable. I held my breath while he smoothed out the skin of my stomach, plastered with a clear gel, accompanied by the low hum of the machine and soon after a–

'Heartbeat,' Neilson belched the word out and smiled. 'A clear, definite heartbeat.'

It took a second to register, though, while I tried to drown out my own that was thrumming in my ears as the blood rushed about my body; every cell just that little bit panicked by it all.

When I didn't answer, Neilson piled on more information. 'I would wager we're looking at about eight, nine weeks maybe? If you look here...' He pointed to the screen and I craned my head around to see. 'If you look just here at this shadowing, you'll see the foetus taking shape. It's hard to get it all, I know,' he sounded disappointed when I looked away, 'but we can arrange for a clearer scan a little further down the line. Right about now, though, your baby is busy making a face for itself so we can't rush these things. Let me just take a quick snap here–'

'Don't.'

He looked bitten. 'You don't want a picture?'

Is it worth back-pocketing this? I thought, then, and nodded instead. 'Actually, do.'

'I imagine it's something Fin will want to see for himself.'

I smiled. 'Yes, I suppose you're right there...'

It wasn't until we were back with a desk wedged between us, once the good doctor had filled out and ticked here, there, that I asked about next steps that were available.

'Well, there's the scan I mentioned, which I think we should wait a few weeks for. But we can book you in for a follow-up scan like the one you've just had, if you'd like to bring Fin back with you and...' He petered out as I shook my head. 'You don't think he'll want to?'

'I haven't been clear.' I leaned forward, as though readying to swap a secret. 'I don't want to continue with the pregnancy. What next steps are available?'

'Walking on Broken Glass', I noticed outside then. Dolores couldn't have picked a more appropriate song if she'd tried. Neilson looked at me open-mouthed, confused; anyone would think I was making arrangements to abort *his* child. There was a pluck of sadness in me, then, somewhere deep down – next to the baby, maybe – that wished I was going to get this moment with Fin.

Neilson stammered out several false starts before admitting, 'I don't understand.'

'Are you aware of the situation with my husband at the moment, doctor?'

He shook his head. 'I'm afraid...'

'He's under suspicion of murder. For killing the man I was having an affair with.'

The second wave of shock looked even worse for him than the first had. He leaned back in his chair and pushed his glasses up to his brow, so he could rub hard at his eyes. 'The baby. It isn't Fin's?'

'Oh, make no mistake it is,' I reassured him. 'But it isn't exactly how I thought we'd be bringing a baby into the world, Dr Neilson.' I tried to sound sad about it, too, and perhaps there was part of me that was. But the part of me that sat in the driver's seat, then, was more concerned with ammunition and long-term freedom than she was about maintenance for life and custody agreements. The former concerns had won out. 'I would like to terminate the pregnancy, Dr Neilson, whatever my reasons for it, and I'm led to believe there's no reason you actually need my husband's approval for that.'

I thought I saw the flicker of a smirk, as though he might be about to disagree with me. But then his face dropped as he realised I was actually right. 'Of course. I understand these aren't the circumstances for... Agnes, you've been trying for so long, though, shouldn't you... couldn't you...'

I'd come to hate both of those words. I slowly shook my head in answer. 'Shouldn't, couldn't. For reasons that are likely obvious to you, I'd prefer if the billing for this didn't go through my husband.' I fumbled with the buckle of my bag and then searched inside for the envelope. 'In there, you'll find details of where to send appointment costs to from now on and–'

'Violet Kent,' he said, questioning.

'Yes, the account holder's name is Violet Kent.' I was careful with my wording. It was Vi's name acting as an umbrella for my money – money that I'd filtered away from my husband diligently over the years. 'Now, if you don't mind, doc, I'd really appreciate if you could walk me through what happens next...'

I dropped my head back against the car seat and took a deep breath. The woman handling Vi's calls had put me on hold with generic music that wasn't conducive to relaxation. But I tried to breathe out slowly rather than let air and feeling flood out in a great gush. I was about to reach for the emergency cigarettes in the dashboard when Vi answered.

'Love, are you okay?'

I sighed. 'I'm pregnant.'

There was a long pause before she replied, 'I see.'

'I'm sorting it.'

'I see.'

'You're judging me,' I spat.

'Quietly.'

I laughed. 'You think I should keep Fin's baby.'

'Christ, when you put it like that... I think you should do what's best for you, love, I always think that. Is being tied to Fin, for the rest of your life, what's best for you? I'd wager against it.' I heard a knock on the door in the background. Vi must have covered the phone because she sounded muffled, then. 'A minute, please. I'll come to you.' Her voice came back clearer when she said, 'Impatient arseholes today, all of them. I'm going to have to go. Why don't you come over tonight? We'll talk.'

'Is there something to talk about?'

There was another long pause, then, weighted and round in the belly. She knew what I was asking.

'I told you not to worry about Cameron,' she eventually said. 'I sorted it last time and I'll sort it this time.' There soon followed another knock, this one louder. 'I'm going to have to go. You're welcome to come over this evening. Call first. But if you want to rest then stay with the coven.'

I laughed. 'You hate them.'

'I hate them. Bye, love.'

I dropped my phone on the passenger seat and pulled my

hand back to sit on my stomach. My fingers curved around an imaginary bump and I rolled around the idea of what it might be like to let myself bloat with life. 'If you're a woman, though, maybe you already understand the horror of that,' I said, either to my child or to no one at all, I wasn't sure. But despite any sadness, the decision was already made: nothing would seal the housewife's revolt like killing the only heir.

CHAPTER TWENTY-EIGHT

E verything was taking too long. The investigation seemed to have slowed. Though Fin wasn't back at work yet – and he didn't have a houseguest anymore, either. Cameron had moved in and out of view of the windows during his stay, but never ventured beyond the front porch. The housewives would have seen, and told me, if he had.

I'd explained him away as an old boyfriend who also happened to be a friend of Fin's; they'd pledged such an allegiance to me by then, though, that I thought I could have told them anything and had it be plausible. Apart from the truth, that is; apart from: 'I nearly killed him, once.' Still, Cameron's visit had lasted days, and all the while I imagined him and Fin swapping notes and scheming. What I'd done to him hadn't been illegal – given the context – but it would have cast something of a shadow over me. Though Cameron's arrival left me wondering if any scars I'd left were deep-rooted enough for cool revenge – or whether he'd hear Fin's wild stories and decide he was better out of it. Of course, there was another option: he'd remember the turn in me, that night, and he'd believe every word – because he thought he knew what I was capable of. Not that either of them really had any idea...

On the fifth morning of Cameron being there, it was Fin who answered the door when a courier arrived. I watched from my makeshift bedroom at Xara's. My breath had caught when Fin disappeared; whatever the delivery was it wasn't for my husband.

Cameron was as beautiful still as he had been years ago, and I wondered how many of his students had seen that in him since. His shirtsleeves were rolled up and his glasses pushed onto his head, sweeping back the beginnings of loose curls that only came when he was that bit overdue for a haircut. When I saw the confusion pull at his face I remembered, only a flicker, of the night we'd spent together and– Knock.

'Agnes, I said Foucault.'

I'd heard his safe word; I just hadn't done anything about it.

Cameron had retreated into my home with a package in tow. Xara saw him leave an hour later; bags packed and all. I sent Vi my thanks in a WhatsApp message that I deleted as soon as the ticks turned blue.

Nicole was back in the village on an overnight trip. She hadn't wanted to stay at the house – the crime scene, that is – and I hadn't wanted to risk bleeding out on Xara's spare mattress, so I'd given up the room in favour of staying at Umi and Jessa's.

'Agnes, really...' Nicole had started to protest but I wouldn't hear of it.

Xara and Dermot still hadn't had any luck with a pregnancy of their own, and Umi and Jessa had never expressed a desire for children. It was the least I could do to take my second dose of pills in someone else's bathroom.

'If you're sure that you're sure?' Nicole asked, in a tone that was suspiciously affectionate given the ties that bound us.

I had been sure, and I told her, twice; I promised and everything. Though I'd needed a failsafe in case the premonition of a bloodied mattress happened to come true.

So, like a crude bedtime story, I asked Umi and Jessa if I could talk to them both before we trod up to bed on the evening of my stay.

With nervous faces they agreed and sat opposite me, their hands clasped together like parents awaiting a coming out. To their credit, I was sleeping in their spare room while my husband, accused of murdering my lover, was holding my home hostage, so I could understand their hesitation. I looked between them both and pulled in a staggered breath for dramatic effect, then gave out a sad laugh.

'I'm in the middle of a miscarriage.'

The lie came easily, though it had been the first one I'd felt guilty for telling. They'd flanked me, then, rushed to my sofa and wrapped arms around me from either side and the affection of it all caused a rise of something in my gut. Still, at least I didn't have to worry about looking uncomfortable; I imagined that discomfort was expected.

'What do you need?'

'Can I get you anything?'

'Do you want to sleep in with us?'

'Jessa, I hardly think that's appropriate.'

Jessa reached around to slap her wife on the arm. 'Don't lower the tone.'

I laughed, though, and said, 'She never gives up, this one, does she?'

Umi gave me a squeeze and answered, 'Not on good friends, no.' She kissed the side of my forehead – it was the first time she'd shown that soft affection with me – then squeezed again.

'Come on, to bed with you. We're a shout away if you need anything.'

The two of them had walked upstairs behind me as though waiting for me to pass out at any moment. They'd stolen more hugs on the threshold of my room and Jessa had lingered for so long that I'd thought of asking her to tuck me in, just to make it easier for her to follow me. But instead I only thanked them and disappeared behind my closed door – where I didn't sleep a fucking wink with the ill-feeling of it all. At some time after midnight, I'd moved from making educated guesses about how many flowers made up the wallpaper, to actually counting them one by one – until I inevitably lost track and forced myself to start over, like a child counting sheep who happened to hop the fence every time I looked away.

The morning after, we sat down for a civilised breakfast together – and I wished to be anywhere else.

'You look rough, doll. Are you sure you're up for this?' Umi said as she sat a bowl of fruit down on the dining table.

'She means to say you look tired.' Jessa squeezed my arm and on the way back to her kitchen she shot her wife a killer glance. 'You can excuse yourself at any time, Agnes,' she shouted in, 'and we can just say you aren't sleeping well.'

'Which would be true.' I laughed. 'How could anyone in good conscience sleep with what's happening, what's happened?' It might have been the sincerest question I'd asked of them. 'I'll be fine, really, I think this will be–'

The front doorbell cut me off.

'–good for me,' I finished, as Jessa moved in and then out of the room to let the others in. Only when she reappeared we were missing a wife still.

Xara's expression was twitchy; she didn't wear nerves well.

'Did Nicole change her mind?' I asked when her and Jessa were both lingering alongside the table.

'Not exactly.' Xara flashed a tight smile. 'The police are here. They, ah... DS Fendley, is it? They wanted to talk to you– Talk to you both, not just *you*, but you and Nicole. I said I'd come to get you, though, and give them... Well, you know, give them some privacy for it all.' There came another smile, then, which I took to be a signal that she'd finished, but more flooded from her. 'They looked as though they might have brought some evidence with them. I, ah...' She petered out and stole a glance at Umi, who only looked back in a startled way and then shrugged. 'I think there's something they want to show you both.' But then she threw her hands back and laughed. 'Christ, what am I saying? I have no idea whether there's something they want to show you both. I...'

'Xara, calm down.' Jessa set a hand on her shoulder. 'Go back, we'll bring Agnes across in a minute. That's all right with you, Agnes, isn't it?'

'Absolutely. Thank you for coming over, Xara.'

'Sorry.' She belched out another nervous laugh. 'There are police, in my house, again. You know? Sometimes the reality of the whole situation really nips at me.'

Try being me. I only nodded and looked away, and they all took it as the sign it was intended to be. Jessa saw Xara to the front door while I struggled from my seat; the blood rush felt like a period bleed and I hoped my pad would hold from one house to another. Though they'd warned me that everyone bleeds differently – which had felt like very late life advice.

I smiled at Umi when I was upright. 'I'm walking like someone showed me a good time.'

She laughed and crossed to me, then offered her arm. 'You're a filthy cow, you are, Agnes.'

'Don't tell your wife.'

'Pah, I wouldn't dream of it. She'd get worried about you.'

Something turned over in me and I felt the need to shift

attention. 'Never mind me; we should all be worried about Xara with the way she's behaving. How nervous the poor thing was just then.'

'Hm.' Umi let out a huff noise. 'Maybe *she's* killed someone.'

I stumbled, lost my footing and felt my knee buckle.

'Easy, easy.' She tucked an arm around my waist. 'Are you sure you're up to this?'

'Of course.' *It'll do them good to see me looking like a victim.* 'I want to help them.'

Umi held my arm as I crossed the road to Xara's house, and Jessa stayed close behind us. Short of a police escort – which I wasn't in a hurry for – I imagined this would be the closest I'd get to security assistance. On the threshold of Xara's front garden, I paused and glanced back at my own home – and I saw my husband's silhouette in an upstairs window. Jessa soon shielded me from it, though, with an arm around my shoulder to hurry me along – 'Don't pay him any attention, Agnes, just don't.' – and we saw ourselves in through the front door that Xara had left on the catch. Inside, she was nervously loitering in the hallway with the same crooked energy that she'd been wearing at Umi and Jessa's house, too. *I'd love for them to suspect you of something,* I thought, then, as I flashed a sympathetic smile.

'They're just through there.' She pointed, and I followed the gesture.

The living room was open just enough to see Nicole seated on one sofa. There was a leg nearby to hers; pressed black trousers that could have belonged to Fendley or Craw, who I couldn't see but could hear clearly enough. I tapped the door gently and pushed – 'Yes?' – at Fendley's reply. And soon I saw their evidence: the blue tie, with a polka-dot print of tight red flower buds that I'd brought Fin for our first anniversary; the same tie again, that I'd bought Eliah after the first hurried time we'd had sex.

Nicole looked between the ties once more, then up at me.

I nodded and thinned my lips into something I hoped looked like sadness.

Finally, they've found it...

CHAPTER TWENTY-NINE

In the days after we swapped late night phone calls about my husband: 'Why hasn't he been arrested?' we all wanted to know, apart from Nicole who had fled the scene again off the back of an especially aggressive albeit entirely understandable outburst.

After I confirmed for the police that yes, I had bought both ties, and yes, it had been terribly bad form to do so, Fendley revealed in turn that both ties had been found in *my* house.

It wasn't altogether surprising, though, given that *I'd* put them both there. I'd worried once or twice that Fin might find them before the police did. But for Fendley's eventual reveal my outward expression became one less of refreshment and more of bewilderment – 'I'm sorry, I don't think... I'm not sure I quite...' – coupled with a gentle tumble backwards, into the arms of my new friends who were ready to catch me and make excuses on my behalf. 'She hasn't been sleeping well,' Umi lied, before Jessa had the chance to say anything more honest; or what she believed to be more honest, at least, which was essentially the truth in many ways now.

'I don't understand what game they're playing,' I said to

Xara during one call. She'd invited me back to hers after Nicole had left but given her new nervous disposition, I thought it was best to give her a break from the drama of it all. Besides, Jessa was a surprisingly maternal host – who plumped pillows and left chocolates behind while I wasn't looking – and Umi was a desperate flirt. They were much more entertaining bedfellows to struggle through the performance with.

'They told Nicole they want to get a firm case in place, Agnes, that's all–'

'Have you seen Fin today?' I interrupted her, and she hesitated to answer.

'I don't know that I have. I'm looking over now, too, and there aren't signs of life. Why do you ask?'

I paused for dramatic effect. 'I'm going to go over and get a few things.'

'Agnes...'

'I know, I know. But you're here and you know where I'm going to be. Perhaps you can just keep a lookout?' I heard a strangled noise creep out of her, and I smiled. I knew Fin was home. I'd seen him pacing in front of the windows since the early hours of the morning; our insomnia as in sync as it had always been. But I knew a nervous lookout would call the police earlier than anyone else might, too. 'I'm just going to get a few things, Xara, I promise. I'm so tired of borrowing from you all. I'll get my things and I'll leave, okay?' I waited for a response and when one didn't come I pushed harder. 'If I'm not in and out in ten minutes then I give you full permission to send in the hounds after me. Is that fair?'

She sighed. 'Christ, I don't like this. But fine, Agnes, fine.'

I ended the call and grabbed everything I might need: my house keys to the back door; a fresh lick of lipstick that he'd likely hate; the ultrasound – and the grit that had made my husband gun for me in the first place. *I'll give them a firm fucking case.*

My concentration was so set on opening the back door in silence, I didn't spot the state of the kitchen until I was two steps into it. I crossed to the table that was covered with strewn papers. *Legal documents?* I wondered, or maybe research on how to kill a wife with no one noticing. But the more I ferreted through the papers, the more I came to recognise the handwriting as my own: it was the hurried scrawl of lecture notes; late night ideas; snippets of research that I'd found in the dead of night during my doctoral studies. My entire thesis was deconstructed and decorated across the table and, when I turned, I noticed it along the work surfaces of the kitchen, too, the island, even across parts of the floor. Fallen papers, I assumed, until I took a closer look and realised they'd been arranged neatly in an order that made sense. There were three and a half years of my life rearranged here, I realised, punctuated by the occasional undergraduate dissertation or masters-level document; things I could remember sneaking under the plagiarism radar, to borrow from work I'd already done. Fin and I had talked about that at the time – 'Everyone does this, Agnes, I promise. You're such a worrier.' – but he'd never asked for the specifics of what I was submitting. He'd never asked about any of it.

I crouched to get a better look at the work that was spread out on the tile flooring, smudged with stains that I couldn't remember leaving. I could imagine my husband pawing at the documents late in the hours of an evening – or even into the early hours of the morning – and the thought gave me a sad-pleasure for a second. *It's too late to take an interest now, Fin...*

'I was looking for a clue.' His voice came from behind me and, while I knew he was in the house somewhere, the abruptness of his arrival really had caught me off-guard. He smirked in such a way that I thought he was pleased about my nerves. 'I can't tell when you're faking and when you're sincere, it seems. Did you really not know that I was here?' He narrowed his eyes and made a clicking noise; I imagined his tongue knocking against his hard palate. 'There either aren't clues in here, or I haven't found them yet. Though whether I've got the time to keep looking is anyone's guess.'

I glanced around at the papers. 'A clue to what?'

'Whether you've always been unhinged,' he took two slow steps into the room, closer to me, 'or whether it's something *I* did for you at some point.' I noted the phrasing: *for* you; not *to* you. 'There's nothing here, though, is there?' With an outstretched arm, he swooped across the expanse of knowledge that was between us still. 'There's absolutely nothing to suggest that you're unhinged because...' He petered out into a laugh and tapped at the side of his temple. 'You're *too* unhinged to go leaving behind clues like that, aren't you?'

'Fin, I've got no idea what you're talking about but–'

'Are you wired?' He folded his arms. 'Is *that* why you've got no idea?'

I opened my arms wide and revealed my torso to him. 'Pat me down.'

He laughed. 'You'd like that, wouldn't you?'

There was an uncomfortable silence between us that stretched out for seconds. We stared each other down as though each we were waiting for the other to call bluff. But when he didn't close the gap any further, I lowered my arms.

'I came to collect some of my things, that's all.'

He stepped aside to clear the way to the door and gestured. 'Be my guest.'

I was going to have to walk past him, still, but I kept as wide a distance as I could. My stomach tensed at the thought that he might grab me en route but he didn't; Fin had always known how to play the long game.

Outside of the kitchen, the house looked pristine – untouched, in many ways. I hadn't seen a cleaner come and go at any point. So whatever explosion of feeling had happened in the kitchen clearly hadn't seeped out into the rest of our domestic spaces. I trod slowly through the living room to take it all in – the colour blocking, the soft throws, the effort I'd gone to – and I imagined how Fin might have filled his time in keeping these nooks and crannies clean. *So maybe he does understand, now, how the inside of a house swells to fill a whole life*, I thought as I rounded the corner to the staircase.

I came to a stop on the landing, though, when I saw the door to a guest bedroom was hanging open. Despite myself, a small laugh erupted like a knee-jerk response. The bed was ruffled, the duvet hanging half on the floor, and there was a sweep of aftershave stepping out of the room, too. Though I'd never spent a full night with Cameron, I'd always imagined he might be a messy houseguest.

'He doesn't clear up after himself, that one, does he?' Fin asked from the bottom of the stairs. I didn't answer, only shook my head and went to move away. 'What's Violet got on him?' And I froze, then. 'Do you even know, or do you just let her do... whatever it is she does?'

'I don't know what you're talking about,' I answered without turning.

He charged up the stairs, two at a time, and I couldn't move anywhere fast enough. I pressed myself up against the wall only to create some distance, but he was in my face sooner than I could find an out. The heat of his breath steamed my cheeks, and I turned my head away as best as I could.

'You nearly killed him, Agnes, did you know that?'

Yes. 'I don't know what you're talking about.'

'Did you kill Eliah? Was it really *you* that did it?'

Yes! 'I don't know what you're—'

His palm collided with the wall at such a force that I wondered whether the plaster might fracture. 'Stupid doesn't suit you, Agnes. Did you kill him?'

I turned my head back, then, only an inch or so, to catch his eye.

'Do you really hate me enough to let people spend the rest of my life believing that *I* did?'

Though of course, none of this was about hate. But like every husband who refuses to let go of his wife, I knew Fin wouldn't understand any explanations that I might give.

'You could have just left, if you were so unhappy. You do know that.'

'No,' I answered quietly; so quietly that his head dipped to listen.

'Okay, well I'm telling you now, Agnes, you *can* leave. You can call this whole thing off and leave. How about *that* for a deal?'

There was a juggernaut that surged up through my stomach, then, and even though it was a medley – nerves, sadness, joy, relief – when it manifested in the cave of my mouth it was laughter: a high and hurtful crackle that even I didn't recognise. But of course it was no deal at all that he was offering me; of course, it was too late to back out from any of it now.

'You bitch.' He snapped. 'You're laughing at *me*?'

I dropped my head back against the wall with a dull thud. 'Us, I'm laughing at us, love. Look at what we've become.' But then I moved closer again, close enough for the breath of my words to knock against the hot anger of his panting, and if we hadn't been so busy thinking of tearing each other apart just then, we might have made love like teenagers right there on the hallway carpet. 'Am I too much for you now, Fin? Too much woman and not enough wife?'

'You're a goddamn psychopath either way, Agnes, a mess just like your mother.'

'My mother's an addict. I'm not addicted to hurting you.' I lowered my voice into a whisper. 'I've just decided that I really enjoy it.'

There was a flicker of movement in my peripheral vision. But I felt his hand close around my throat before I knew that's what I'd seen. *Once more for old times' sake*, I thought as I felt the pinch of him. His palm was pressed hard against my larynx, to squeeze the living voice out of me in much the same way as he had during the rest of our marriage. I didn't struggle to be free of him, though; I only relaxed into it. After seconds of pushing against me, he eased away and leaned forward with his lips instead. Softly, his mouth knocked against mine and I let him have it; I could feel how much he wanted it all for a moment: it was almost like he loved me, still. He nearly eased his hand away entirely, as he pulled back and took a good look at me. The warmth of his fingers wasn't far enough away for me to believe he'd changed his mind, though, and I knew it might all still work out.

'Tell me you don't love me,' he said, then, and I was stunned. 'Why?'

He shrugged. 'Maybe I'm just trying to understand.'

'I don't not love you, Fin. But I don't love our life.'

'So change our life,' he spluttered.

I whispered again, 'I have.'

He grabbed at me like you'd grab the arm of a child about to walk into oncoming traffic. He snatched and pushed and I would have coughed if I'd been able to get the sound out. Fin tucked his fingers either side of my neck, pulled me towards him, then slammed me back, and I felt the first hard impact of the wall. He was busy spitting accusations – 'You're a monster, Agnes, a goddamn monster...' – while I was stretching for the back pocket of my jeans. I tugged the ultrasound softly, yanking free one corner at a time so he didn't notice. But when he slammed me back again, pushed hard on my throat and laughed as he felt the ripple of the cough move through me in a near gag, I let the image tumble to the ground like a dying thing during a season change. Someone would find it, I reasoned, and it would be a perfect accompaniment to the– Knock. He threw my head back again and the pain shifted through my skull like a wave shifting from back to front and I thought, *He might really do this*. I locked eyes with him because I wanted him to watch me die through this – but I wanted to watch him, too, husband of mine. I wanted to watch while he kneaded and pushed and– Knock. I wanted to swallow but even that felt too much under the weight of him. And suddenly there was a warmth, not in my throat but my pelvis; the warmth that comes with spilling over the side of your liner during a heavy flow. And I wondered whether they'd find me bleeding as well as dying and– Knock.

'Answer me, you bitch!' he shouted, but I hadn't heard a question.

The blood was rushing about between my ears; a tidal wave trapped in a jar and all I could hear was myself, thinking, *This might be how it*– Knock.

'Dr Villin! Dr Villin, it's–'

There was a final grab and smash and then he leaned in and I felt the heat of all his anger and disappointment and–

'Is this what you wanted, Agnes? You wanted it all to catch up with you? Well you win, you get what you fucking wanted.'

'Dr Villin–'

'DS Fendley, I've found–'

'She wanted this, she wanted me to catch up with her in the end!'

'Agnes?'

'Finian, get off her now and–'

Knock.

There was a light. It flickered in and out, and on the other side of it there was a young woman who I didn't recognise. Her hair was pinned in a tight bun. And every time I opened my eyes there she was, peering at me from the other side of the flash. There was something on my face, too, that felt uncomfortable, like a pinch over my nose and mouth at once. But when I moved to shift the thing away the woman behind the light touched my hand gently and moved it back to my side – 'Agnes, you need to leave that where it is, my darling, okay?' – and then she stepped into the light again. It took another four deep breaths to realise she wasn't behind the light, though, but holding it. She was lifting one eyelid, then the other, then the other. Like a spasm I fluttered both lids at once then and blinked into the sunlight that was behind the woman – 'That's my girl, there you are, Agnes, another couple of deep breaths.' – and suddenly noise rushed in like someone unmuting a television, and I reached for the thing hugging my face again and again the woman pushed my hand away.

'That's helping you to get some air in okay, Agnes? You were starved of a little oxygen there for a while and we're trying to get some air back in your lungs, my darling, okay?'

Starved of oxygen? I tried to remember but– 'Talking is going to be uncomfortable for a little while, too, so don't feel that you have to try just yet. But I'm going to hold some fingers up and can you try to match the fingers I'm holding, by holding up your own?' She tapped my hand, as though I mightn't understand where my fingers were anymore, and I tried to nod. 'Good girl, okay, ready?'

She held up three fingers in my eyeline, silhouettes with sunshine blurring their edges. I matched her. And for every flash of hand that came after I matched her, and then I struggled to swallow and–

'Okay, my darling, swallowing will hurt, too.' She moved my hand away from my neck and I wanted to ask her to stop touching me but the words were nesting in the back of my throat and when I tried to cough it felt like–

Oh. 'Fin,' I managed, my hand around my throat like a bandage that could protect me from the bruise of speech. 'Fin.'

The woman turned away and spoke to someone off-screen. 'She's asking for her husband. Can we...' I didn't hear the response that came, only saw her nod and then turn back to me. 'Agnes, Fin isn't here, okay? You're safe, and we can't really say anything more than that at the moment, my darling, but you're our main concern now anyway.'

'Animal,' I heard someone say; the person off-screen, I guessed. And I wondered whether they meant me or my husband.

Xara was apologising in my ear and by then delirium was at such a high I wondered whether she was the one who'd choked me. I wasn't quite upright, but they'd removed the face mask – hung it loosely around my neck like a Halloween accessory – and adjusted the gurney so I could look out the open doors of the ambulance.

There was fussing and shoving and– 'Please, please I'm the one that called the police for her. I'm her *friend.*' I'd heard

Xara's voice ring clear despite the distance between us. She'd given the word 'friend' more weight and bearing than I thought it deserved but I wasn't in a position to protest; I still needed them to believe all of the magic tricks I'd shown them. So when she tumbled into my sight line full of apologies – 'Agnes, I was just *so* worried, and time was going on, and I didn't know what to do.' – I flashed a faint smile and beckoned her towards me. She gave me a gentle hug as though I might fracture under the touch of her – but if my husband slamming my head into a concrete wall hadn't knocked me off my feet then Xara seemed an unlikely candidate for such a job. Again, though, I only faintly smiled. I sensed that in the coming days there would be a lot of faint smiles and weary expressions; I was readying to swoon when I saw the rest of the coven who were–

'Excuse me, we're her bloody neighbours for a start and friends, first and foremost I'll have you know.'

They were closer than I'd realised.

'Agnes, is there anything you need?' Xara asked, huddled awkwardly inside the ambulance with me. There were so many bodies and not enough space, and when I tried to answer I found that my voice still couldn't carry over it all and–

'She's going to struggle speaking for some time, I'm afraid,' the woman had to speak for me. 'Agnes, I'm going to step out for a moment and let your friends stick their heads in before they cause a ruckus out there.' She smiled and I tried to match the gesture. 'You'll only have a minute with her while we get the area cleared and then we'll have to take her in,' she explained to Xara, who nodded furiously and then moved aside for the woman to leave.

'Agnes.' Xara pushed damp hair away from my forehead. 'Christ, what did he do?' Then she waved the question away. 'Rhetorical, I know you can't...' She gestured to her throat then went back to stroking my hair.

'Aren't you a sight–' Jessa slapped Umi's joke away before she could finish it. 'I'm obviously yanking her leg.'

'Well, don't.' Jessa crouched into the limited space that the woman had left behind and she grabbed my hand. 'Are you okay, lovely Agnes?'

'She can't talk,' Xara leapt in with the excitement of someone who has insider information. 'Her throat... She can't...'

Umi disappeared, then, and I wondered whether it was the lack of conversation that had done it for her. Jessa and Xara carried on fussing, though, filling the space with coos and shushes and blasting Fin's character and–

'Agnes, my darling, I'm just going to lift this blanket away for a minute.'

The woman was back, with Umi, and–

'Is she in there? Is she in that fucking ambulance?'

I thrashed and fussed and threw myself about at the sound of him. I behaved exactly like a woman who'd nearly been killed by her husband. And my friends – my beautiful stupid friends – behaved exactly how I expected them to.

'She's in here miscarrying your child, you bloody brute!' Umi announced to the world but there wasn't time enough to hear his response because then Xara spoke and the woman and Jessa, and all at once they were covering me up like a gallery piece not fit for public viewing and then the woman said we needed to leave.

'Now, come on, everyone move it!'

In the days after, whenever I woke up there was a different face waiting to greet me: Xara; Umi; Jessa. But Violet was never far behind any of them. They'd fought to wrangle me into their empty nests where they could fuss and pamper me. But Vi, clever and domineering Vi, had said that for the sake of my sanity if nothing else it would be better to get me out of the village. 'This is a neutral space, love. You can be whoever and whatever here, and you're safe all the while.' She cooed variations of the same sentiment every night while stroking my hair and waiting for me to drift into sleep. But she'd been accommodating with the many visitors; the women who'd left their cosy homes to venture into the city on alternate days. It was five days later when they all came at once and Vi arranged catering for a lunchtime gathering, too, but every swallow set me wincing and I imagined it was an unappetising sight to be positioned opposite.

I looked over at Umi who was watching me struggling to eat pastry. 'I'm sorry.'

'For?' she answered, plainly. 'I'm a middle-class lass who went to an all-girls school, you think this is the first time I've watched someone struggle to eat pastry?' She winked, then threw a mini quiche into her own mouth in a single bite. 'You've nothing to apologise for, Agnes,' she spoke around the mouthful.

'Unlike my wife.' Jessa handed her a napkin. 'Who seems to have forgotten that we're in fresh company and shouldn't behave like animals.'

'Please.' Vi waved away the worry. 'I actively encourage women behaving like animals.' She closed the gap between her and Umi by leaning in across the table. 'Don't you think the world would be a better place for it?'

When Vi was upright again I softly tapped at her arm. 'You're terrible.'

She had to lower her head and lean in to hear me. My voice was one of the few things she'd forgotten to pack up when she ventured into my marital home, and I was still speaking at a whisper.

'But I'm making you laugh, aren't I, love? And that's about all I can prescribe for you at the moment.'

But as I laughed I lurched forward: something had spilled out of me. The doctor – who knew that I had aborted my baby – said that the added stress of the attack might bring on a period, or cause extra bleeding from the medication. 'All sorts of potentially unforeseen side effects, I'm afraid.' And she really had sounded sad about it. Since then, I'd left blood stains in three different spots of Vi's home and she'd expertly cleaned away the evidence, with the stomach of a woman who either spills too many clots a month or has a more colourful sex life than I'd given her credit for – but it wasn't the time to ask which of the suspicions were true.

We locked eyes together and she gave me a knowing glance, rubbed my knee under the table, and went back to amusing the wives. It felt like I was introducing my husband to a new round of girlfriends – and Vi was excelling in the role. She told me to stay seated as the desserts came to a close and after she'd kissed their cheeks and welcomed their hugs and seen them swiftly out the door, she came back into the dining room looking exhausted.

'Let's get you cleaned up, shall we?'

'I'm sorry,' I answered. My only sincere apologies were the ones I issued to Vi.

She held out an arm for me to lift myself up with. 'You swipe that smut from your mouth. There'll be nothing like apologies in this place.'

I showered while she tended to the ruined dining chair. Then, like a respectable mother and guardian, she suggested setting me down for a sleep. 'It's been a long afternoon, love, don't you think?' she asked, guiding me into the room I'd now adopted as my own. She led me slowly to the bed, peeled back the covers and let me lower myself comfortably onto the mattress. It was observable in her own features, how hard this was to watch, and it was the only time I'd felt guilt for what I'd done.

'Anything you need?' she asked, her head close to me, ready to catch an answer.

'Cameron...'

She laughed. 'No, you certainly don't need him, love. Those sedatives are–'

'No.' I shook my head and felt it sink back against the pillow. 'How did you...'

'Ah.' She nodded. 'You'd like a bedtime story?' She didn't wait for an answer; only disappeared from the bedroom and then came back a second or two later, holding a thick and weighted manila folder. She set it on the bedside table and dropped back onto the bed. 'It doesn't make for pleasant reading, but there's everything. The first time around I got rid of him by reminding him that an early academic researcher shouldn't be fucking students.'

She nodded to the folder, then, and added, 'This second time I reminded him of much the same. Of course, it's worse now he isn't an early academic researcher. He's older, the girls are younger.' She sucked in a greedy breath. 'And his tastes changed after you. He became... more hurtful. I'm not sure how else to say it. Other than to add that he wasn't much of a receiver anymore. More of an inflictor.' She smiled and pushed a stray wave of hair back behind my ear. 'The thing is, Agnes, men like Cameron never do just make one mistake...'

Vi and I sat hand in hand like expectant parents in her living room. DS Fendley wasn't presenting us with a gender reveal, though, so much as a firm and court-ready case. For Eliah's murder, there was an eyewitness in my good friend Jessa, who was more certain than ever – strangely – that she'd definitely seen Fin walking near Eliah's house and heading back towards our own on the day of the murder: '"Bloodied and agitated" is the phrase she used,' Fendley said and I only nodded. Then there's the motive, which isn't evidence in itself although it certainly didn't look good. Couple that with his penchant for strangling – 'Yes, I'm sure I'm happy for the images to be used in court.' – and the fact that he can't produce an alibi that holds any weight. 'For a time it looked like his colleague, a Dr...' she hesitated while she looked for the name. 'Irene Loughty, I believe, it looked as though she were coming down on his side, but she was elsewhere at the time, she realised, on reflection.'

Atta girl, Irene, though I kept my face neutral at the news. Fendley told us, then, that his alibi had been the last thing they were waiting to crack – only hours before they stormed our home. 'Then there's the tie...'

The tie that happened to be the same print as the one I'd bought Fin. I'd bought Eliah the same by sheer coincidence. I shook my head. 'I just liked the print.' I shrugged. 'It didn't even occur to me that I recognised it from somewhere and now... I just feel so stupid now that–'

'Agnes, don't,' Vi instructed. Then she urged Fendley to continue with the details.

'It was boxed at the back of your husband's underwear drawer.'

'Christ,' I tried my best to sound disgusted. 'Why would he even...'

I asked – because I knew it was the question everyone else would ask, too. Nothing about Fin or his crime would explain a trophy like that. But I was wise enough to know we wouldn't have gotten far without it...

'The why is something we'll have to thrash out as we go, I'm afraid. I'm led to believe he's got a defence, of sorts, though that's not something I'm at liberty to discuss here.' *I'll bet he'd got a wild defence at the ready*, though I nodded slowly in passive understanding to everything she said. 'Really, Agnes, I'm probably telling you too much as it stands. But after everything you've been through, I... I feel you've a right to know some of this. It's off the record entirely.'

'We understand, Violet, don't we?' She nodded in support. 'And... I know it's an ask, perhaps, after all this already, but my own case?'

She smiled, in a sad and reserved sort of way. 'Two police officers watched your husband try to strangle you, Agnes. I think the charge of attempted murder, or more likely manslaughter, is certainly going to be a hard one to dispute. There's no defence against what we saw.'

'I... I appreciate that, DS Fendley, thank you.' I squeezed Vi's hand and then stood, slowly; I was still recovering, after all. 'I'm sorry, can you excuse me for a minute while I use the bathroom?' Vi went to stand with me but I paused her. 'I'm okay, really.'

The bathroom was two doors down, but I lingered outside the living room door. I couldn't risk missing anything of worth, and I suspected there were one or two things the good detective wouldn't want to say in front of a healing and withered victim.

'I imagine he's spouting a sprinkler of shit about Agnes already.' Vi was the first to break the silence, and I heard Fendley splutter a laugh. 'I'm sorry, detective, I'm not one for beating around the proverbial.'

'I appreciate that.' There was a pause, where I imagined Fendley scanning around to the doorway to make sure I wasn't playing spectre. 'Despite the advice he's being given, he seems to be leaning on the lie that Agnes has somehow framed him for Eliah's murder, and that really she's the one we should be suspicious of.'

There was a long pause before Vi said, 'And can he prove that?'

'I think you and I both know the answer to that. But you know I can't–'

'Foul play on my part, my apologies. I'm sure the jury will see how Agnes, with a pearl necklace of bruises, a voice that drops in and out like a poorly wired radio, and what is, in my professional opinion, the beginnings of PTSD from having been strangled by her husband, I'm *sure* they will see how she's the threat.'

I sighed and smiled and waited. I imagined Fendley smiling in a similar way.

'I'm sure you're right.'

I folded and tucked the scarf like I had a hundred times before. Only now, I was covering something that everyone knew was there. The bruising was fierce; purple and angry for weeks. Xara had offered to try to cover it with make-up when I'd mentioned my plans to venture out into the world. Umi had said it wasn't worth it, given that everyone knew already. In the end it was Vi who drove back to the village to collect the wardrobe of scarves that I'd become so dependent on throughout my marriage already. She stood behind me in the mirror while I tried one then another then another, until finally settling on one we thought matched my outfit. Though she left me in privacy to put the finishing touches to myself.

Beyond my room – or rather, what was by then my room at Vi's – I could hear the chirps and laughter of the women, and I thought of how desperate Vi would be to wash them off later. She tolerated the wives for me, but in private she made no secret of the fact that she believed these weren't my people. Still, they'd all gathered for the occasion, to support me through choosing an outfit and deciding whether I was anywhere near as ready as I thought I was for what I was planning.

'Well...' I span into the room wearing a knee-length bottle green skirt with a white shirt, open-collared, neatly tucked into my waistband. I was wearing a patterned green necktie, too, with orange flecks in the swirls and circles of it that I hoped might bring out my eyes. 'Do I look like a woman you'd–'

'Yes,' Umi and Vi answered at once.

'You didn't let me finish.' I pouted.

'We don't need for you to,' Xara chimed in, 'you look fabulous.'

'Better than fabulous.' Jessa stood and crossed the room to hug me. After a tight squeeze, she bowled her palms around my shoulders and held me at arm's length. 'What you look like, Agnes, is a free woman.'

CHAPTER THIRTY

I t was bold, going for a job interview at Fin's university. Only it wasn't his university by then, and any close friends he may have once had had fallen down the cracks when he'd been charged with murder and attempted manslaughter. It would be reaching to say they'd welcomed me with open arms. There were some who still observed me as Fin's wife; I could see that much in the way they sized me up in the hallways. But there were also some who seemed to think of me as redemptive somehow, and that made them kind and accommodating in ways that academia hadn't been the last time I was a part of it. I'd been working there for nearly a full month when Irene and I crossed paths, too.

'I am sorry,' she said plainly. I'd walked past her as though she were a stranger, but she pulled me back with the apology, and as opening sentiments went I had to give her credit for a strong move. When I turned to face her, she repeated it: 'I'm sorry.'

'Whatever for, Irene?' I raised an eyebrow. 'My understanding is that he had you fooled as well.' She went to add something more but I shook my head. 'We really don't need to do this. Neither of us have clean hands; neither of us have hands as filthy as my husband's. Let's be thankful of that and live out our lives, shall we?'

Her mouth bobbed open and closed two times, like a dumbstruck goldfish. But instead of settling on something verbal, she nodded, slowly, and then smiled.

'I'll be seeing you, Irene.'

'Agnes.' She turned and hurried along to her side of the campus. And I watched for a few seconds until she rounded the corner out of sight, all the while wondering what it was my husband had seen in someone quite so plain. *Maybe* that's *what he'd seen in her*, I thought then, over a montage reminder of what his last colourful love interest – namely, me – had ended up doing to him.

I finished treading the distance from my Monday morning lecture theatre back to my offices where the next proverbial hurdle was waiting for me: Shawna. Or, as I was now trying to think of her: Mum. I flashed her a tight smile and nodded towards my door. She wordlessly stood and followed me. To say that we were on friendly terms would have been a stretch of the imagination. But we were on speaking terms at least. And we had been since news of Fin's behaviours had gone national in terms of media coverage.

Mum hadn't reached out to me then, but she had to Vi. There had been a taut phone call that ended in Vi covering the speaker and reminding me that flies preferred honey to vinegar, and since then Mum and I had spoken once a week. I didn't want her as a friend. But from the last I heard Fin hadn't yet retired the party-line where he accused me of being a mastermind murderess. I reasoned that having Mum as a character witness *against* me wouldn't be ideal. And knowing that husband of mine, I wouldn't have put it past him to call her and at least ask.

'Take a seat,' I told her as I dropped into an ornate chair on my side of the desk. On my first week here I'd raided Fin's office for the best of his furniture; the chair had been the last thing I'd taken, after the bookshelves and a globe that turned out to have four bottles of alcohol hidden inside it. My husband had been a clever man, sometimes. 'It's really nice that you've been able to see the campus.'

She looked around the room and her eyes landed on the high ceiling. 'Look at this place, Agnes. You've done...' I heard the sentiment catch in her throat, and the glug as she tried to swallow it again. 'You've done so well, and your father would be so proud, especially under... Well, correct that, now, the circumstances have nothing to do with it. It's amazing, under any circumstances.' Then she shook her head abruptly as though remembering something. 'Especially under the circumstances that I put you under as well, Agnes. Don't think that I've forgotten, forgiven... I...'

In the time we'd been talking, we were yet to mention steps or rehab or the numbers of days since an incident. But from the pinched colour of her cheeks I knew she wasn't drinking – at least not today – and from the guilt in her I knew that in those moments at least she meant what she was saying. So a favour for a favour, I gave my mother what she needed – in order for her to believe I was a good daughter.

'I do forgive you, Mum.'

Like a house of cards caught in the wind, she folded in on herself one limb at a time until she was huddled and crying in a small mound opposite me. She shook with such feeling that I began to wonder whether I'd said the wrong thing. But soon the tears gave way to the shoulder shudder of laughter, instead.

'You must think I'm loopy.'

Yes. I shook my head, though, and answered, 'I'm guessing it's relief.'

'It is, it's such a relief, Agnes, and I–'

My desk phone chirped into life and I was grateful that something had cut her off. I leaned over to check the ID.

'I'm sorry, Mum, it's Vi. She's...' I tried to make it seem like it was hard to say. 'She's at court today. There was talk of... I don't know, there seemed to be talk of a plea for Fin and... I'm sorry.' I set my hand on the phone, but I didn't answer.

She wiped under her eyes. 'You didn't want to be there?'

Be there? I'd put *him there.* 'Vi offered and...' The phone was still ringing so without any further tension building I snatched the handset up. 'Sorry, Vi, Mum's here and...' I petered out when I heard the hustle of the background, the click and whir of media. I imagined Vi fighting her way to be free of the meddling crowds, past the groupies that were lining up to write letters to my incarcerated husband. Assuming he *was* still incarcerated.

'Agnes? Agnes, love, he's bloody given in and done it.'

I knew that Patrick had passed along the advice to take a plea option. But in my lucky stars I never really believed *my* Fin would roll over. Unless I really had broken him – or perhaps prison had, already.

Vi lowered her voice for the next part, and I imagined how she must have cupped her hand around the phone to protect the words, too: 'You did it, Agnes. You got away with it.'

It had been hard to keep the truth from her...

'Everything okay?' Mum whispered from across the desk, and I nodded.

'Vi, that's bloody brilliant news. We must celebrate.'

'Already ahead of you, love, I'll book somewhere and send–'

'I don't need a car,' I interrupted her, and laughed. 'Tell me where you've booked and I'll meet you there from work. And thank you, again.'

'Any time.'

She disconnected the call so I dropped the phone back in place. 'Guilty times two,' I told Mum and she smiled, but it was a sad expression, too. 'I know, it's a strange sort of sensation, isn't it?' *Relief, suspicion still, maybe something like smugness*, I quietly tried on the words for size before sharing, 'Sadness, even guilt.'

'You did nothing wrong,' she said, quickly, as though I'd kicked her in the back of the knees with the mere suggestion. 'Fin had *everyone* fooled, Agnes, it wasn't just you; it wasn't just anyone. He's... Well, I wouldn't like to say what he is.' She leaned forward in her seat and rested her hand palm up on the desk between us; I took the cue and matched the gesture. She squeezed, smiled and said, 'But you really *are* free from it all now, Agnes, and that's what you must hold on to here. You're safe and you're free.'

I nodded, slowly at first but then with more gusto. 'I'm safe and I'm free.' She smiled again then and rubbed her thumb rhythmically across the back of my hand while I chanted her words, 'I'm safe and I'm free. I'm safe and...'

'The world's your fish dinner, isn't that what your dad would say? The world's your fish dinner, our girl, and with everything you've already done, well, whatever will you get your teeth into next?'

I leaned back in my chair, took in the sight of the office around me, and thought: *Well, Shawna, isn't that the question...*

THE END

ACKNOWLEDGEMENTS

In the wider writing community – especially the online writing community – I've met some of the best people I know. I'm fortunate, too, to know so many brilliant Bloodhound Books authors who offered support throughout this book, and throughout others. I'm forever in the debt of the digital world of writing that offers so much, story after story.

Given the content of *Safe Word*, there were some risqué internet searches done to get everything just so in Agnes' narrative. There were also some really generous friends involved, too, who I won't name, but I will thank, wholeheartedly, for helping me to understand, learn, and get the details right. I remember one friend telling me she was glad I was trying to write about Agnes' kink(s) with a level of accuracy: I hope that's what I've done here.

A final thank you to my ARC group, for always volunteering time to read, and to anyone who read the blurb, picked the book and settled down with it: I hope you loved reading Agnes as much I loved writing her.

A NOTE FROM THE PUBLISHER

Thank you for reading this book. If you enjoyed it please do consider leaving a review on Amazon to help others find it too.

We hate typos. All of our books have been rigorously edited and proofread, but sometimes mistakes do slip through. If you have spotted a typo, please do let us know and we can get it amended within hours.

info@bloodhoundbooks.com

Lightning Source UK Ltd.
Milton Keynes UK
UKHW041359141222
413922UK00015B/186

9 781504 077842